# The Legend of Decimus Croome

# A Halloween Carol

## by Kevin Purdy

Purdy Books
Louisville, Colorado 80027

Contact **www.PurdyBooks.com** to receive teaching/learning guides for using this book in the classroom and for information about upcoming publications. Please follow PurdyBooks on Pinterest, Facebook and Twitter.

If you think *The Legend of Decimus Croome* would make a good movie or graphic novel, please sign the petitions at:

**http://www.ipetitions.com/petition/decimus-croome-the-movie**

**http://www.ipetitions.com/petition/make-legend-of-decimus-croome-a-graphic-novel**

# Table of Contents

# Chapter 1 - The Legend Lives

Tommy teetered on the tips of his toes in order to peer over the nearest gray-green tombstone in search of his sister Kate. At first he could see nothing but a scattering of cobwebbed headstones of various shapes and sizes.

He began to read a barely legible death poem on one of the larger stone markers when suddenly he heard a voice bouncing from gravestone to gravestone, sounding distant and peculiar.

"Tommmmyyy." His sister's voice, oddly muffled, was just loud enough to startle him but not loud enough to penetrate beyond the black spiky fence that imprisoned the cemetery and all those within it, both living and dead.

At the sound of his sister's voice, Tommy simultaneously ducked down and stepped backward. His foot came to rest on something round, hard and brittle that cracked under his rather unsubstantial weight. He wasn't positive if the cracking sound came from whatever he stepped on or from his own ankle. He felt a sharp pain just above his left foot as he fell back into an awkward and clumsy sitting position on the ground. He was pretty sure he had only twisted his ankle, but he could already feel it beginning to throb as images of a shattered bone momentarily flashed through his mind.

He still couldn't see his sister, but he had the strangest feeling that he might not want to see her. From the sound of her voice, he was sure that she had changed. After all, it was that time of year and soon everyone would be making the annual transformation. For that reason and many more, he was hesitant to look down to see what he had stepped on. Instead he slowly reached toward the ground with one spider-like hand while still scanning the stone garden that surrounded him.

He quickly discovered what he had stepped on, and it was just about the same size and weight of a large stick except it was relatively smooth as if the bark had been stripped away. He cautiously brought it up to eye level, still afraid to look down. But as soon as he realized what it was, he let out an involuntary bellow and threw it toward the ground.

Forgetting his sister and his creepy surroundings, Tommy summoned the nerve to look down at all the white stick-like objects that littered the ground all around him.

Some of them lay randomly here and there with no discernible pattern. Others were stacked in small piles like a campfire waiting to be lit. But many of them seemed to be arranged to form a more familiar shape. They seemed to be an outline of something Tommy recognized but couldn't quite put his finger…

It all became frighteningly clear. The outline was familiar for a reason. He was looking at the outline of something very recognizable indeed. The sticks formed the shape of a human body… a skeleton. Because they weren't sticks at all. They were bones. Human bones of all shapes and sizes. There were rib bones, leg bones, arm bones and even finger bones scattered everywhere. And he was standing right in the middle of them, surrounded by them. They looked like they could come to life any moment and grab him by the leg to pull him down into the bowels of hell.

Tommy's eyes remained locked on the bones as he tried to stand up and make an escape. But there was no escaping. The bones were everywhere and he couldn't help but step on them as he moved backward. He felt another sharp pain in his left ankle and heard a crunching of bones underfoot and once again he began to fall backward, off balance both physically and mentally. He reached out his hand hoping to find something to grab; hoping to stop his fall and provide support.

Sure enough, his hand struck one of the nearby tombstones, but it provided no support. He watched in horror as it tottered and began to fall. He expected to hear a crash or at least a loud thump as it shattered to the ground. Maybe he would hear the sound of more bones crunching under the weight of the ancient stone. But there was no sound at all. No crunching, no thumping and no crashing.

And although the gravestone toppled silently, Tommy's plunge was less dignified. His legs seemed to crumble beneath him, and he let out a grunt as he crumpled to the ground, his arm still reaching for support, his ankle sending out lightning bolts of pain.

From his awkward ground level perch, Tommy noticed more oddities that he had ignored before. The bones were still the most noticeable feature that met his eye. But now he also noticed a scattering of colorful fall leaves and a thick net of cobwebs stretching up to a gnarled old tree trunk. And where there were spider webs, there were spiders.

Sure enough, as Tommy surveyed the tangled labyrinth of silken strands, he began to notice the familiar black dots of creepy crawlies. When he gazed upward, he noticed hundreds of spiders of varying sizes in the cobwebs and on the ground nearby with some of them spilling over onto the neighboring tombstones.

Tommy began to rise from his humiliating fall when a movement caught his eye. It came from a few yards away, behind another one of the tombstones. At first he assumed it was his sister but, if so, something was radically different. The lone figure turned away from him, so he wasn't sure at first, but then he recognized the green jacket with white stripes. It was similar to the one that Kate had been wearing earlier. And the silent stalking silhouette looked to be about the same height as his sister.

But for all the similarities, there many striking differences. Her straggly hair looked miscolored and completely disheveled. As he looked closer, he realized that splotches of hair were missing altogether revealing ugly, reddish patches of bare skin. It looked more like the scalp of a sickly ninety year old than his vibrant teenage sister.

Tommy reached down and curled his fingers around one of the larger bones that lay nearby. He brandished it like a club as if some instinctive survival mode had awakened inside his head. He had no idea what he feared or even if he had reason to be afraid. But he wasn't going down without a fight.

When he glanced back up, he realized that his sister had begun turning around to face in his direction as if she had read his mind or heard him pick up the makeshift weapon. As she turned, Tommy noticed that her face was ghastly pale and distorted. It seemed to be covered with scars that never existed before, and some of the scars looked almost as if they had stitches running through them. The changes in her facial features were chilling.

Tommy lay perfectly still as his sister's gaze scanned somewhere slightly over his head. He had never felt so vulnerable and exposed, with nothing to hide behind. He drew in his breath and tried to remain dead still as she seemed to look directly at him. Now he could see her entire face, and he didn't like what he saw. Where there was once beautiful, unblemished skin, there was now a number of jagged lacerations. Her previously angelic smile was replaced with a cracked-lip grimace. And her hideously protruding eyebrows seemed to be pierced with some type of small spike or large thorn.

Every survival instinct within Tommy's brain screamed at him to flee; or at the very least, to look away. But he couldn't. He was frozen both out of fear and out of wonder. He couldn't help but stare at the hideous face on his sister. Was it still his sister? When does a person stop becoming a person and devolve into a creature? What is the boundary between natural and supernatural?

Why wasn't she acknowledging him? It seemed as if she was staring right at him. Or was she staring right through him? And why did her dreadfully transformed face look more fearful than frightful?

Then Tommy realized that she was looking neither at him nor through him but slightly above and beyond him. She seemed to be looking at something that was every bit as disgusting to her as she was to him.

Whatever it was, Tommy didn't want to see it. He didn't want to turn around for fear of seeing what may be lurking behind him. He was suddenly filled with a fear much greater than what he felt when he saw the tombstones or boneyard or even his newly zombified sister. He was absolutely positive that whatever his sister was looking at, whatever was behind him, was not something he wanted to see… now or ever.

Against all common sense, against every instinct, Tommy very slowly began to turn around, his eyes glued to the ground hoping that nothing would be looking back at him when he mustered the courage to look up. His sister was probably just being dramatic. She was probably just trying to scare her little brother by pretending…

Tommy detected a slight movement and heard the raspy sound of labored breathing coming from straight in front of and above him. Then, he saw an impossibly large and tattered pair of brown shoes, so scuffed and worn to the point that jagged holes penetrated the frayed leather revealing a pair of grayish-white socks underneath.

Somewhere from high above the dilapidated shoes Tommy heard a muffled, grunting noise but he resisted the urge to look up at the source of the sound since he had no desire to see what the shoes were attached to. Tommy's first impulse was to run, but by the time he got to his feet and took his first step, whatever loomed above those big feet would have him in a death grip. He turned his head to look back at the zombie that seemed to have replaced his sister.

Despite the distance between them, Tommy noticed the dry, pallid complexion on his sister's face. But what startled him most were her eyes. Her dark brown pupils were so large, they stood out against her pale, eroded skin, and they seemed to be trembling. She looked even more fearful than Tommy felt.

Escape was out of the question at this point. So he gritted his teeth, swallowed a deep breath and slowly turned back around to face the shoes… and whatever menacing creature was looming above them.

The first thing he saw, directly above the tattered old shoes was a gargantuan pair of legs that seemed to stretch skyward like two gnarly old tree trunks. The legs were covered in a faded pair of overalls that looked almost as gray as the surrounding tombstones but were probably black at one time. An assortment of patches, haphazardly stitched on, covered a series of holes in the pants. Tommy's mind immediately imagined a gruesome story to explain each of the patched holes; one was from a gunshot wound, another from a snarling werewolf, yet another from a slashing ogre.

Tommy's imagination skidded to a halt as one of the towering legs took a step toward him, and another rumbling growl shook the air. Tommy tried to get to his feet but only fell backward and was forced to gaze up at the rest of the beast's torso long before he was prepared to do so. And now it was his turn to growl, but he could only manage a feeble yelp.

Over the years, dark tales of Decimus Croome had circulated among the impressionable young children of Timberton. As the years melted, one into the next, the legends grew horns and fangs and tended to surface in sleeping dreams and waking nightmares. Each year, the legend grew darker, and children spoke, in hushed tones, of how unimaginably horrid and rotten was Decimus Croome. The murmurings and mutterings grew even more freakish and grotesque as Halloween slithered ever closer. For that was when the legend of Decimus Croome seemed to expand like a parasitic beast feeding off the lifeblood of the town's children.

And when young Tommy Bobbich peered skyward, it

was that very same infamous Decimus Croome who towered over him swaying like a rotten old oak tree in the wind. A natty red-checkered flannel shirt covered his apelike arms stopping just short of his meaty and gnarled paws. One of the hands was balled into a fist while the other was holding what looked like an enormous axe that seemed to Tommy as if it may have once belonged to Paul Bunyan.

Tommy almost began crawling away from the towering hulk when he saw his sister cautiously approaching. He wasn't sure if this was good news or bad news. Now Croome could add two new notches to his axe handle rather than just one. Despite this gruesome realization, Kate's courageous approach bolstered Tommy's confidence somewhat. On the one hand he didn't want to see his sister get pulverized any more than he wanted to become another Croome statistic himself. But what could he do? What could Kate do? Even the two of them wouldn't stand a chance against this mammoth marauder.

Tommy was mortified when he saw his sister advancing on Croome, but he was even more horrified when she confronted him. "What are you doing here...?" Her question was stopped in mid-sentence as one of Croome's meaty hands reached up and ripped off Kate's face.

---

Croome stood looking down on Kate and Tommy, an axe in one hand and a crumpled zombie mask in the other. Tommy was still nervous about Croome but was relieved to see his sister's face had returned to normal. He much preferred her princess phase over her latest zombie fascination. Clammy pale didn't exactly look good on her.

Croome stood over them looking crankier than ever and held up the notch-less axe that now looked somewhat less intimidating. "What does one usually do in a hardware store?" The cranky colossus grunted, not used to pesky children asking him questions. "What are you two doing cavorting around this… this…" He surveyed the expansive hardware store with a look of disdain. "…this god-awful flea-market without adult supervision?"

"Tommy and I were just looking at the Halloween decorations while our mom…"

"And does your father know that his family is

patronizing..." Croome's face took on a look that was even sourer than its usual permanent scowl as he scanned the cavernous warehouse. "... the Home Emporium." He spat the words out as if they were poison.

Just then, Mrs. Bobbich strode around the corner with a shopping cart full of cleaning supplies and Halloween decorations. "Okay kids. I got everyth…" Her face became almost as pale as Kate's zombie mask. "What in the world?" She looked from her children to Decimus Croome to the fallen Styrofoam tombstones and scattered plastic bones.

Belinda Bobbich knew Decimus Croome only too well. She had heard many of the rumors about him and realized that most of them were highly exaggerated. Despite that, she was not his biggest fan. Her dear husband and father to her children, Sam Bobbich, had been a loyal employee at Croome's Hardware store for many years. So Belinda Bobbich knew just how cranky, belligerent and miserly Decimus Croome could be.

Before Mrs. Bobbich could speak, Decimus Croome cast a disdainful glance in the direction of her shopping cart. "I see you are a loyal supporter of the Home

Emporium, Ms. Bobbich. Maybe you don't know about the generous discount that I provide for my employees and their families?"

Unlike her kindly husband and half the townspeople, Belinda Bobbich was not intimidated by Decimus Croome and his sarcastic comments. "As a matter of fact, I am quite familiar with the two percent discount that you offer **ALL** of your employees." Sam Bobbich was, in fact, Croome's only employee, and Croome's minuscule discount still did not bring the Croome's Hardware prices as low as the Home Emporium. But Mrs. Bobbich decided not to mention that. "But since Croome's Hardware doesn't sell Halloween decorations nor cleaning supplies, I find it necessary to shop at the places that do."

"Yes well, as you know, I run a hardware store, not a holiday store." Croome now cast a bitter glance towards the Bobbich children. "Or a playground."

Mrs. Bobbich was accustomed to such comments from her husband's employer and chose to ignore them. She glanced down at the axe in Croome's hand. "But I do believe Croome's Hardware sells axes, last time I checked."

Croome's grizzled old face turned a barely noticeable

shade of pink, and he shot a guilty glance around the store to make sure no one else was eavesdropping. "A slight correction Mrs. Bobbich. Croome's Hardware would sell axes if its employees would replenish our stock every once in a while."

Belinda Bobbich knew that Croome was infamous for blaming her poor husband for all of the ills of Croome's Hardware, and she wasn't about to stand for it. "Another slight correction, Mr. Croome. Your employee would be glad to replenish your supplies if his boss didn't insist on stocking only one of each item and only allow the purchase of new supplies once every month."

The look on Croome's face was nearly as repulsive as the monster masks that lined the nearby shelves. "Well I would love to stay and chit-chat but, at this very moment, my neighbor's maple tree is protruding over *my* fence and dropping its pesky leaves onto *my* property. As usual, I'll have to do all the work and chop the branch down myself." Croome shouldered the axe like a lumberjack and abruptly turned toward the front of the store.

"Well a happy Halloween to you too Mr. Croome." Despite her best efforts to remain cool, Mrs. Bobbich was fuming. "And have a merry autumn while you're at it." She snarled to the receding Croome.

She took a moment to compose herself and then turned to her two children. "And what is the meaning of this mess?" She pointed to the fallen tombstone and broken bones. "Apparently I can't leave you two alone for a minute." She glared from Kate to Tommy and back again to Kate.

Kate knew better than to argue. Just a few minutes earlier she had pleaded with her mom to trust them to be on their own in the store. The last thing she had said to her mom was, "I'll watch Tommy while you finish your shopping." Then, when her mom had paused to think about it, Kate added, "We'll be fine. Don't worry about us."

Now Kate knew that her mom was way beyond worrying. She was furious. Worse yet, she was furious in a public place, and was about to make a huge scene. Kate would have almost preferred to face the wrath of Old Man Croome rather than be publicly humiliated by her mother.

Fortunately, Tommy came to the rescue. His lip started quivering and tears welled up in his eyes. He let out a little sob, then whimpered, "Mr. Croome scared us. Why was he so mean?" Tommy held out his arms and limped toward his mom whose demeanor quickly changed from grizzly bear to mama bear as she scooped Tommy up in a big hug.

"Oh Tommy. Mr. Croome isn't mean. He's just a…" She struggled for the words. *bully, jerk, cranky old fart.* Was what she wanted to say. " …frustrated man who doesn't always communicate well." Was the best she could come up with.

Then she turned her attention to Tommy's limp. "Are you okay? What's wrong with your leg? Why are you limping?"

Kate was concerned about her brother both physically and emotionally. She didn't know that he'd been so frightened by their recent encounter. She knew he had been extremely weak lately and that their parents were very concerned about…

She couldn't bring herself to think about Tommy's illness. She tried hard to act tough and invincible, but she couldn't bear to think about her brother's recent trips to the hospital and the looks of concern on her parents' faces. She knew he was becoming more fragile each day, but she had no idea that this run-in with old man Croome would make him so distraught.

About that time she noticed that her little brother was glancing in her direction, his chin resting on his mom's shoulder, his recently acquired baseball cap tilted awkwardly on his head. He flashed Kate a huge smile then a stealthy wink. Unbelievable. Just when she was feeling sorry for the little imp. He had totally saved their bacon.

"I don't know what you think is so funny young lady." Mrs. Bobbich gently lowered Tommy to the floor, careful not to put too much weight on his injured ankle. "First you shirk your responsibilities and make a mess in the store, then your little brother is scared half to death. I don't see anything funny about it. Now unless you want to be grounded for the rest of the month, you'd better get this mess picked up. And no more monkey business or you can forget about trick-or-treating and Halloween parties."

Again, Mrs. Bobbich shot her daughter some major stink-eye before turning her attention back to her injured son. Once she was sure he was going to be okay, she began pushing her cart toward the front of the store.

As Tommy gingerly walked by Kate, trying hard not to

limp, he held his right hand behind his back with his palm up. Kate slapped it and muttered under her breath, "You are good. Where did you learn that?"

Tommy turned to face his sister then winked at her and whispered, "From an ugly zombie I once knew."

# Chapter 2 - Decimus Croome

Halloween was dead, and nothing could make Decimus Croome happier.

More precisely, nothing could make Croome happy. He was a cranky soul made even crankier by the mindless exuberance of the blasted holiday season. Decimus Croome hated all holidays, but he absolutely and positively despised Halloween most of all.

Rarely one for maudlin sentimentality, Croome cracked the faintest trace of a smile when he contemplated the demise of Halloween with its campy costumes, copious candy and cacophonous cavorting. It was enough to give the crusty old malcontent heartburn whenever he flipped the calendar from September to October. Of course one must have a heart in order to suffer heartburn, and many in the town of Timberton would have sworn that Decimus Croome was the most heartless creature that ever trudged upon the face of their planet.

So what was it that made Croome smile on this particular Halloween Eve? What could it be that turned his usual frown into a grimace of pleasure? Of all things to make him smirk with malevolent pleasure, it was the most unlikely visage that transposed his typical scowl into a somewhat disturbing grin.

Of all the unlikely sources of Croome's delight, it was the insidious Christmas decorations that caused him to grin from cheek to cheek. By no means was Croome a fan of the inane Christmas displays that were cropping up a little earlier each year in every single store across the town. But if the trend continued, the red and green rubbish that seemed to litter every storefront and clutter every local business would soon eliminate the vomitous orange and black of Halloween. And that, my friends, was what brought a rare grin to Croome's face. The demise of Halloween made the cantankerous curmudgeon simply bubble-headed with delight.

But Croome's rare delight was clouded by his recent confrontation with the moronic Bobbich family. The kids were bad enough with their ridiculous Halloween masks and despicable displays of public misbehavior. But Croome was especially appalled by the mother, Belinda Bobbich. One would think a responsible parent would know better than to let her children run loose in a public place of business. Why if those spoiled kids behaved that way in his store…

---

Decimus Croome was in the hardware business having inherited the family store many miserable holidays ago, and he made it a point to visit his competition once each month to see what ridiculous baubles adorned their shelves. Croome's Hardware had been a fine business in the days of old, but two dreadful diseases were hastening the demise of Croome's Hardware store specifically and community hardware stores in general. One particularly nasty assailant was the dreadfully distasteful big-box home improvement warehouses. Croome's Hardware store could easily fit within the holiday section of the local Home Emporium hardware giant. Their selection was greater, their prices lower and their pedantic pandering employees in their purple aprons were oh-so polite.

Always the realist, Croome could accept the inevitable competition of the insidious hardware behemoth. It was business, and business was all about competition. Croome knew that he had only to continue catering to his few loyal customers for a couple more years when he could eventually sell the family business and retire to a peaceful existence of tinkering and gardening. He dreamed of a life with no customers, no employees and no worries.

But there was another challenge that Croome could not overlook. In recent years, the hardware business had taken a dangerous detour in a dreadful direction. Now most people wouldn't consider this new turn-of-events to be so dreadful, but Croome cringed whenever he contemplated it.

Decimus Croome was a second-generation hardware store owner. Back when his father opened Croome's Hardware, that is exactly what they sold… hardware. If a customer needed hammers, nails, saws or lumber, they visited Croome's or any other local hardware store; and they would more than likely find just what was needed to fix a faucet, repair a roof or even build a barn. And the same was true when young Decimus took over the family store.

But more recently, much to Croome's eternal dismay, hardware stores evolved into a completely different beast.

No longer did they peddle just hardware. In fact, most of them weren't even called hardware stores any more. They were now called home improvement stores; and home improvement meant home adornment and home adornment meant namby-pamby knickknacks and imbecilic embellishments. And the worst season of all was in full swing as old Decimus Croome made his way down the jam-packed aisles of his archrival, the Home Emporium.

---

"This place looks more like a circus sideshow than a hardware store." Croome mumbled, narrowly avoiding a collision with two young teens careening out of control toward the detested holiday displays. Few things made Croome angrier than careening teens. Every bone in his body ached to stick his arm out and clothesline the two young troublemakers. He cracked another rare smile at the thought of the speeding demons twirling around his beefy arms and landing with a thump on their rumps.

Croome's face began to ache with all of the unaccustomed smiling before it effortlessly resumed its more familiar scowling. Exactly half of his rage was directed at the two young hooligans who had obviously mistaken the store for a playground. The rest of his resentment, however, was directed at the infernal holiday displays. "Is this a *home improvement store* or a toy store?" he had once asked the store manager before stomping away without awaiting an answer.

Croome bypassed the rapidly expanding Christmas display and headed straight for the dwindling Halloween paraphernalia. He would deal with Christmas later. For now, his rage was directed toward the ridiculous ghosts and goblins that currently haunted the aisles of Home Emporium.

As Croome rounded the corner leading into the bowels of Halloween kitsch, he was accosted by a particularly nasty mechanized troll whose garishly green head popped out at him with ogling eyes and a probing proboscis. Most startling of all was its wicked sounding mechanical voice that scared the bejeebers out of Croome. "I thought I was supposed to be the one with the scary face!" Cackled the troublesome troll with an annoyingly mechanized voice.

Or that's what it would have said. But as soon as it said

"I thought I was supposed..." a startled and grumpy Decimus Croome lashed out with a wicked right-hand-cross into the green-and-black gnarled troll face putting a violent end to its pestiforous Halloween greeting once and for all.

Croome stared sheepishly at the mangled troll head that bobbed to and fro on the display shelf like a drunken cobra. He quickly glanced around, hoping his pugilistic outburst hadn't been witnessed by any of the busybody customers or purple-aproned employees. He didn't want another embarrassing mishap like the one he had last year when he had been escorted from a local grocery store for a similarly antagonistic incident involving an animated witch that had dared to wish him a happy Halloween.

As he turned back around, he collided with the same young hooligans who had accosted him earlier. Only this time, they had covered their irritating little faces with even more irritating Halloween masks. Croome was in no mood for Halloween hijinks. He was already fit to be fried and feeling much uglier than the most hideous Halloween costume in the store.

With his usual disregard for civility and tact, Croome

extended one hefty paw and, while the dashing young demon was in mid-stride, collared the young hellion by his oversized vampire cape. With the shining black cloak in his left hand, he grasped hold of the young hooligan's Dracula mask with his massive right hand and twisted it 180° so that the eye sockets were in back. The satanic young sprinter continued scurrying along at warp speed, his vision now completely obscured by the backside of his mask, until a clearance-priced riding lawn mower abruptly halted his forward trajectory.

Croome furtively glanced around and smirked, "Pest clean-up in aisle three." Then he mumbled to himself, "Who needs a stake through the heart when you've got lawn tractors?"

Next Croome bent down and placed his hand on top of the youngster's backward mask. He not-so-gently turned the boys head so that he could direct his comments into one of the ear holes of the dumbfounded young lad who sat swaying back and forth next to the clearance lawn mowers. "Now repeat after me," Growled Croome. "No more running in stores."

After a few moments of stunned silence, the temporarily

blinded young miscreant began howling like a hound from hell. Croome took this as a sign to beat a hasty retreat. Rounding a particularly sharp corner, he toppled an end-cap of scarecrows then nearly plowed into the diminutive partner of the young felon he had just accosted. Dressed in a superhero costume and armed with more courage than common sense, the young fellow blurted out, "You're in for big trouble mister. Don't you know you're not supposed to pick on little kids."

Before Croome could come up with a pithy answer, the boy fired another question at him. "Do you know what our teacher said about bullies?"

Croome was caught off guard. "I'm not sure that I care what your teach..."

"Do you know what they do to bullies like you?"

Croome had about had enough questions from the sanctimonious little marauder. It was his turn for a question. "Do you know what they did to Socrates when he asked too many questions?"

The lad was temporarily dumbstruck. "Who is Socrat..."

"Oh, Mr. Smart Fellow isn't so smart after all." Croome mocked. "Don't they teach you kids anything in school these days?"

Not to be dissuaded from his righteous mission, the boy stomped right up to Croome, looked him in the eye and said, "I'm telling my dad that you're picking on us. He's stronger than you and he'll pound you into the ground and then the police will take you to jail." He turned away from Croome in search of his father.

This turned out to be a bit of a mistake for the pious little costumed crusader who had obviously spent too much time around reasonable adults. Before the youngster could take so much as a step in retreat, Croome reached out and grabbed the sanctimonious half-pint by the nape of his costumed neck and deftly hefted the pint-sized ghoul all the way up to eye-level. Gone was the smug smirk on the child's face, replaced by a bug-eyed look of sheer terror.

Without another word Croome stretched out his arm, as if the youngster was as light as a leaf, and hung the self-righteous youth by his superhero utility belt on a display wall of chattering skeletons. Now, with one Halloween reveler wildly flailing his legs in mid-air and the other spinning like a slow-motion top in the garden department, Croome hastily retreated from the cursed establishment.

He had enough experience with such incidents to realize that angry parents and busybody store employees were unlikely to see his point of view regarding the costumed cretins.

Croome hastily ambled toward the nearest exit and, once outside, made a beeline toward his own beleaguered business in order to check on his one employee, a Mr. Samuel Bobbich, to make sure he didn't try to close the store so much as one minute early. This was despite the fact that Sam Bobbich was about the hardest working employee anybody could ever wish for and had never once tried to leave early in over fifteen years of employment at Croome's Hardware.

When old Croome arrived at the store, Sam was sitting behind the cash register, diligently counting out the day's profits, or lack thereof. As always, he smiled at his boss and wished him a good evening.

"Pish-posh on your good evening Bobbich." Croome grunted. "I have yet to see one thing good about it. What have you done with all the customers? Have you scared them off on this miserable Halloween Eve?"

Now a less forgiving and more spiteful person than Sam

Bobbich might have turned this around on Croome and pointed out that if anyone was likely to have frightened away the customers, it was the gloomy Croome himself. But this was not in the nature of meek Sam Bobbich. "It was another slow night, Mr. Croome. A couple people came in asking about Halloween decorations..."

As soon as he had spoken, Bobbich regretted it. He knew that his boss would unleash a torrential tirade.

Croome rounded on poor Sam Bobbich with fire in his eyes. "Halloween decorations? Does this look like a Halloween store to you Bobbich?"

"No s..."

"Does the sign out front say Croome's Halloween Store? Or Croome's Cursed Costumes or Croome's Holiday Nonsense Outlet?"

Now Sam Bobbich was flummoxed and made his next tactical error. "No sir, I sent them to the Home Emporium Mr. Croome."

It was a mistake.

Sam Bobbich knew it was a mistake as soon as he uttered the words. But it was too late to suck them back in, one sorry syllable at a time. All he could do was cringe behind the cash register and wait for the storm to pass.

"You sent them to the Home Emporium? You sent them to..." The look on Croome's face was much more frightening than any Halloween mask currently donning the local store shelves. His cheeks were flaming red, his eyes glowed with rage, and venom shot from his gaping maw. "You sent them to the Home Emporium? Do your realize Mr. Bobbich that every customer you send to Home Emporium is another nail in the coffin of Croome's Hardware? Do you realize that with each passing day, we are losing more money?"

"But you see Mr. Croome...."

"The only thing I see, Mr. Bobbich, is a store that is on its last leg; and a store employee who does not seem to realize how tenuous his position is at that store. Do you realize that the doors of Croome's hardware will soon be shuttered and you, my lugubrious employee, will be begging on the street corner instead of gainfully employed by this fine family institution? It's bad enough that you send your bothersome family shopping at the good-for-nothing Home Emporium..."

Just then, the bell over the door rang, thus saving poor

Sam Bobbich from further tyrannical rantings from his oppressive employer. He quickly dashed toward the front of the store with meek mumblings about gladly helping the customer.

"Be sure you don't send them to the competition, Mr. Bobbich!" Decimus Croome shouted to Sam's rapidly receding backside.

As it turned out, the next customer wasn't a customer at all, but Croome's son-in-law, Darren Tate, a pleasant fellow who often acted as an intermediary between Croome and his daughter, Eve. Always a pleasant sort, Tate was willing to face Croome's acid tongue in order to try and keep peace in the family.

"Good day, Sam!!" Darren clapped a beaming Bobbich on the back. "How are you on this fine fall day?"

"Couldn't be better, Mr. Tate. What brings you and this handsome young man into the store today?"

Young Kellen Tate followed closely behind his father and peeked around his legs at Sam. "Daddy broke our rake." Then he disappeared behind his father's legs again.

"Well you've come to the right place my fine young fellow. I think we've got a rake or two somewhere around here." Sam winked at Darren and started walking toward the display of gardening supplies.

Croome listened to the dribble that passed for conversation between his son-in-law and Bobbich. He had absolutely no desire to make small talk with Darren Tate, but young Kellen was a slightly different story. Somewhere, in some hidden corner of his calloused old heart, there dwelled the slightest inkling of a desire to see his grandson.

Maybe it was just curiosity, possibly just a minor case of indigestion, but some wee little glimmer of sentimentality pulled stubbornly at his heartstrings. Whatever it was, he was determined to make it look like an accident, so he grabbed his clipboard and began to walk slowly up the gardening aisle of his namesake hardware store, glancing from the clipboard to the shelves as if taking inventory or some other clipboard-related activity.

"Well hello, Mr. Croome." Hailed the ever-jovial Darren Tate. For even close family members referred to the patriarch as Mr. Croome rather than his first name of Decimus or, heaven forbid, some maudlin title such as Father or Dad. "I see you've decided to stick with the same Halloween decorations as last year."

Darren was the only person willing to attempt sarcasm or humor of any kind with the dour old Croome. Most people knew that it would only be greeted with approbation and grumbling. But Darren didn't seem to care. For he was one of those rare people who spoke his mind and damned the torpedoes.

"So are you here to buy something, or did you just come by to distract Mr. Bobbich?" Croome scowled at his son-in-law.

"As a matter of fact Mr. Croome, I stopped by to see if you wanted to join us for the annual neighborhood Halloween party? The kids missed you last year and, although she would never admit it, I believe your daughter would have enjoyed seeing you there, too."

"A Halloween party? What in Sam Hill is a Halloween party, and what exactly does one celebrate at a Halloween party? Is it a werewolf's birthday, a mummy's bar mitzvah or perhaps a witch's wedding anniversary?"

Darren was surprised by neither Croome's rejection of his offer nor his sarcasm. "No sir. I don't believe we're celebrating any of those things but, as you know, Halloween is rather a special holiday for your daughter."

Just then, little Kellen Tate popped his head out from behind his dad's legs. "Kids have a habit of enjoying it also." Darren said, looking down at his son.

"Yes," Croome was no longer interested in discussing a Halloween party he had no intention of attending. "That is all well and good. But do you realize that you have a gremlin hiding behind your leg?"

Darren couldn't help but smile. It was the first humorous statement he'd ever heard come out of Croome's mouth. Granted, it wasn't very humorous, but for Decimus Croome it was a stand-up comedy routine. Tate glanced down at his son. "It's been so long since your grandpa has seen you, he thinks you're a gremlin." Despite Croome's attempt at levity, Darren couldn't resist getting in a little dig.

Kellen looked up at his father, then at Croome. Suddenly, with the total abandon of youth, he let out a loud, "Grampa!!!" and ran as fast as his Lilliputian legs could carry him right over to Croome and wrapped his even smaller arms around his grandfather's tree-trunk legs.

Croome was at a total loss for words. He awkwardly reached down and patted the young lad on top of his head.

"Now there's a fine young fellow." Croome stammered, sounding temporarily and inadvertently dumbfounded until he recovered and sternly added, in a much Croomier fashion, "But we don't run in the store. That's how things get broken."

Darren Tate just shook his head. He never ceased to be amazed at what a cold duck his father-in-law was. He noticed his son was looking up at his grandfather with a puzzled and slightly hurt look on his face, so Darren decided to try and change the mood a bit. "I was just asking your grandpa if he would be joining us for our Halloween party."

Again, Kellen gazed up at the gruff grandfather towering over him. "Yeah, Grampa, will you come to our Halloween party?"

Croome paused ever so briefly, for he knew of his daughter's affinity for the blasted Halloween nonsense and all its ridiculous traditions. A fleeting vision of Halloweens past squirted through Croome's cranium and just as quickly oozed out his left ear.

"Halloween? Pish-posh!! It's the last day of October and nothing more. Now if you would like a hammer or a box of finishing nails, Bobbich here will gladly show them to you. Or possibly he'll send you to someone else's store to purchase them, an annoying habit he has picked up recently. As for your Halloween party, please wish everyone a ghastly evening or whatever it is that one wishes at such gatherings. Now good Evening, Mr. Tate." He paused to look down at his grandson. "And you have a wonderful Halloween party too." With that characteristically cranky speech, Croome abruptly retreated to the dark recesses of his store.

"Well, Darren..." Both his sorrowful voice and pitiful visage indicated that Sam Bobbich was embarrassed and dismayed by his boss's callous disregard for familial traditions. "I'm sure it will be a very fine party. Your Halloween gatherings have a wonderful reputation around the town."

Tate smiled appreciatively at the ever-pleasant Sam Bobbich. Sometimes he wondered how the sensitive and caring gentleman was able to tolerate his spiteful boss. "Thank you, Sam. I believe Mr. Croome just made his feelings about the party abundantly clear. But we would be honored if you and your family joined us for the fall festivities."

Sam smiled a truly genuine and grateful smile. "We look forward to your party every year. Tommy loves your Halloween decorations and insists on going for walks past your house, even on the coldest fall evenings."

Darren's smile quickly turned to a look of concern. "How is young Tommy? I'm so sorry to hear about..."

"Oh, Tommy's doing..." Sam paused for a moment, torn between the truth and reality. "Tommy is doing as well as can be expected. The doctors say that he's a tough one, and we're hoping for the very best. Everyone in the town has been so kind, and folks at the hospital have really been supportive too. All we can do is keep Tommy in our hearts and ask others to do the same. But, of course, that goes without saying. Everyone has been so helpful. None of this has been easy for..." Sam paused, then looked down toward a random shelf and began absently moving items to and fro. "... for Tommy and Kate and their mother. But the people in this community have been so generous."

"You know that any one of us would be glad to help you in any way possible. Please don't hesitate to ask."

"I know you would Darren. That's exactly what I mean."

Sam's eyes glistened as he turned away. "We are fortunate to live in a community of wonderfully caring people."

Just then, Croome emerged from the store's back office and stomped his way to where the two men were carrying on. He had overheard portions of the conversation but had no idea what they were talking about. He had just seen young Tommy, and the youngster seemed fine. A bit pale perhaps, but most children seemed pale around Croome.

"No wonder this place is losing money." Croome barked in the general direction of Sam Bobbich. "I don't pay you to stand around and chat with every Tom, Dick and Darren that walks in off the street."

Lesser men would have reminded Croome that he barely paid his dedicated employee a living wage anyway. But Sam Bobbich ignored the comment as he handed young Kellen the rake that his father had just purchased. He walked the two Tate gentlemen to the door and waved goodbye as they ambled down the nearly deserted sidewalk leading away from the store.

Sam soon began the evening ritual of closing the store. Once he had finished, he poked his head into the back room where Decimus Croome was bent over a pile of paperwork stacked haphazardly on an ancient wooden desk. His voice was hesitant and fearful as he addressed his boss. "Sir, I was wondering..."

"What is it Bobbich?" Croome's voice was gruffer than usual, making it even harder for Sam to ask a small favor.

"Yes, I was wondering if maybe I could leave just a little early tomorrow so I can go out trick-or-treating with my son, Tommy?"

"I know who your son is, Bobbich. Do you think I'm some kind of an idiot?"

"No sir." Bobbich knew it was a rhetorical question but was never quite sure when his employer expected an answer.

"Why should I let you off early? Who would mind the store? Do you think we can just close early whenever we feel like it and expect to stay in business? Do you think the Home Emporium will be closing early?"

Numerous possible answers sprung to the mind of Sam Bobbich. Or, more appropriately numerous questions like: What customers? Why can't you mind the store since you don't have any plans for Halloween? Why do we need to be open on Halloween night when we don't sell anything remotely Halloweenish?

But of course the congenial Sam Bobbich didn't ask any of these questions because... well because he was Sam Bobbich and he was talking to Decimus Croome.

"I understand, Mr. Croome." Sam wasn't given to mistruths, but this one just seemed to be the only thing to say. "Would you like me to help you lock up the store?" It was the same question he asked every night even though he knew full well that Croome would never trust anyone with his precious store keys... including faithful Sam Bobbich.

"I think I can handle it." Croome growled. But as Sam prepared to make his exit, old Croome grumbled the kindest thing he had said all year. "Come in an hour early tomorrow, and I might consider letting you go home an hour early."

At first Sam wasn't sure he had heard correctly. He turned back to his boss with a puzzled look on his face. He knew better than to ask Croome to repeat himself. So his puzzled look turned slowly into a tentative smile. He knew one hour wasn't much of a sacrifice. But for Decimus Croome, it was an unexpected allowance.

Sam's tentative smile turned into a radiant beam, and he

stopped just short of groveling. "Thank you sir. I'll be here first thing tomorrow."

"You'd better be." Croome growled. "And don't make this a habit. Next thing you know, you'll want to be leaving early for Valentine's Day and St. Patrick's as well."

Sam faintly nodded his head in agreement and nearly sprinted out of the store before Croome changed his mind.

Ever the mistrustful one, Decimus Croome made one last check of the cash drawers and rattled each door in the dreary old building to make sure nothing was left ajar. When he was satisfied that each penny was accounted for, and the store was sealed up as tight as a sarcophagus, he began his nightly sojourn home.

As with most years, the evening before Halloween was a frigid one, and a slight breeze was blowing. Croome snorted with disgust as he passed house after house decorated in Halloween regalia. "What a waste of electricity," he mumbled as he glared at the ones illuminated with various shapes of Halloween lights.

"Good Evening, Mr. Croome." a smiling neighbor greeted, as they passed on the sidewalk.

"Seems awfully cold to me." Croome responded,

without looking up to see who he wasn't communicating with.

# Chapter 3 - Black Magic

Croome deftly maneuvered past an obstacle course of annoyingly rambunctious children and irritatingly chatty neighbors as he approached his own nondescript home. If he paid any attention at all, he would have noticed that it was beginning to make the transition from quaint old bungalow to creepy derelict house. The lack of upgrades was even more inexcusable considering Croome's daily access to discount home embellishments.

The cement on Croome's walkway was cracked and heaving and his dormant lawn was a dull brownish-yellow. On each side of his large old house, the drab yellow paint was peeling in some spots, cracking in others and completely missing in yet others while at least two of the window shutters hung askew.

As soon as Croome got home, he cautiously navigated the creaky old steps up to his front porch. He cast an overhead glance at the dusty crop of spider webs that adorned each corner of the porch rafters. A lone spider stared crankily back at him, seemingly annoyed at the disturbance.

As Croome extracted a set of house keys from his pocket, he noticed that his daughter had made her annual fall visit. Hanging from a hook on the front door was an old, faded Halloween wreath of dusty oranges, drab yellows and faded browns. "One of these days I'll have to take down that hook so she can't hang that blasted bauble from my door," Croome muttered, indignantly.

Croome made the same pact every year, but he knew he wouldn't follow through. For deep inside the old crank was a sputtering candle of decency and hope. Despite his ill-tempered ways, even Decimus Croome clung desperately to fleeting flashbacks and nostalgic glimpses of happier times.

As Croome unlocked the front door and began to turn the knob, something about the wreath seemed almost as if it had come alive. Old and tattered, it was held together with pipe cleaners and glue. The wreath certainly wasn't much to look at, but it whispered secrets of Halloweens past and sacred family memories. It was a fragile circle of faded silken autumn leaves, the type that ubiquitously littered the aisles of craft stores far and wide. It fluttered lightly in the breeze, making a barely perceptible scratching noise as it scraped against the old door.

Halloween creatures both friendly and gruesome peered out of the rustling leaves. A grimy ghost hovered above a smiling scarecrow that looked puny next to an oversized bat being watched by a wicked witch who was entangled in the web of an even larger spider that was in danger of being eaten by a bug-eyed owl that peeped out of the faux foliage, much more nostalgic than scary.

Croome tried hard not to look at the wreath as he turned his key in the lock and turned the big brass knob. He tried, but something caught his eye as he began to open the door. Maybe it was just the wind, maybe it was the rapidly fading daylight, but some of the wreathly inhabitants seemed to change shape and move. Some of them seemed to shimmer and shift as if they had come alive when he inserted the key.

"Pish-posh and poppycock!!" Croome grumbled as he quickly slid into the house and slammed the door behind him. "All that idle chatting with bumble-brained loafers has made me light headed. A good night's sleep will set things right."

Croome began removing his coat to hang it on a hook by the door when he was seized by an involuntary shiver that rattled his old bones and made him reconsider. "Dratted cold weather. Now, on top of lazy employees and meddling relatives, I'll probably catch my death of pneumonia."

He slipped his coat back on and drifted into the kitchen to prepare an evening meal; the same evening meal he had prepared every single night since his daughter had moved out many years ago. One slice of toast, a bowl of broth, two celery sticks, two carrot sticks and a cup of tea. The carrots were from his own garden and the celery as well. If he couldn't spend time tilling his precious soil, eating vegetables from it was the next best thing. He would just as soon switch his ears with his eyes as vary his evening routine. The routine itself was every bit as nourishing and comforting as the actual meal.

After his usual repast, Croome's mood improved, but only slightly. He was always mindful of keeping his spirits in check lest they soar unreasonably high. As he shed his jacket and prepared to hang it on the door hook, a warm body slithered between his legs and caressed his calves.

"Aaah, my old friend Black Magic." Croome bent down to pet the sleek ebony cat that deftly wrapped itself around his lower extremities. "No doubt you're after some food."

"Yowwww." The usual response from Croome's feline friend.

Predictable. That's what Croome liked about Magic. She was predictable and uncomplicated. As long as he fed her and kept her warm in his large and looming old house, she was satisfied. She provided measured doses of affection and expected no more in return. She ate the same meals at the same time each day. She was there for Croome but expected little more than regular meals and an occasional stroke of kindness. And best of all, she was a lady of few words.

After feeding Magic and turning off all the downstairs lights, Croome flicked a switch on the stairs, hoping to shed some light on his nightly ascent to the second floor bedroom. But as soon as the switch was engaged, Croome heard a pop and saw a flash of light. A low growl of irritation escaped his throat. He hated autumn, he hated Halloween and he despised uncooperative household fixtures.

What he didn't hate was the dark. In fact he had a slight affinity for dark hallways and dusky staircases. Gloom was fine, but pitch black was better; except when spelunking the cavernous stairwell up to his bedroom. In such instances he needed at least a glimmering glow to guide him safely up the creaky stairs to his bedroom at the top, and he wished he had purchased one of the ridiculously cheap flashlights from the Home Emporium. And he probably would have if he hadn't been so distracted by all the young hooligans running around the store.

He knew however that wishing would get him nowhere. "Wish in one hand and spit in the other and see which gets full faster." It was a quaint little aphorism he had learned from his grandfather. "I'll change the blasted bulb in the morning." He muttered to no one in particular, as he haltingly felt his way up the somber staircase.

Halfway to the top, a shimmering shape caught his eye. As he turned to gaze upward, a familiar yet hideously unfamiliar sight loomed before him. The first things he saw, on the highest step, was a well-known but long forgotten pair of boots once worn by his dearly departed father. Then, directly atop the boots was a pair of faded and tattered old blue jeans that once covered the knob-kneed legs of his beloved Grandpa Croome.

He immediately recognized the frayed cuffs and patched holes and the cherished gold watch chain dangling from the pant's pocket. Still further up, he clearly saw his grandfather's old flannel shirt, complete with pipe stem protruding from the breast pocket. Croome even imagined he smelled the faint aroma of cherry-scented pipe smoke and the stronger scent of fresh cut sawdust that he associated with his two patriarchal progenitors.

However, his warm fuzzy trip up nostalgia lane ended there. For atop the aromatic attire sat what looked like a burlap sack stuffed with straw and topped off with a faded old, brown, floppy-brimmed hat that appeared to have been passed down from one generation to the next and was much worse for the wear.

In the shade of the drooping wide brim, Croome could make out a hideous face on the burlap bag. The face was that of a wretched scarecrow, but it was unlike any scarecrow Croome had ever seen. For the lips had been drawn… no, sewn on with red thread as if someone had decided to design a scarecrow with a permanent scowl. Above that was a brown nose that was also sewn on, but with clumsy stitches that ran every which way looking all the world as if the creature had been involved in a gruesome auto accident and been thrown through the windshield requiring a team of surgeons to stitch up the damage.

Finally, just below the hat brim was a slender pair of eyes. After the chilling mouth and nose, the eyes were rather plain, just two thin lines. Croome couldn't tell if they'd been stitched on or drawn with permanent marker. Croome stared in morbid fascination, even though he knew better than to do so. The rational Croome knew he should look away but the curious Croome couldn't help but gaze trancelike directly at the previously inanimate scarecrow.

The scarecrow eyes slowly opened from a slit to a crack and suddenly, without warning, beams of light stabbed outward from them. And when they opened all the way the light was brighter than anything Croome had ever seen. It was like thousands of laser beams were piercing out of an old tattered burlap sack. More precisely, they looked akin to the blazing fires of hell concentrated into two thin shafts of light.

Croome let out an involuntary screech and nearly fell down the few stairs he had just ascended. He instinctively reached for the handrail and grasped it with a death grip that almost splintered the banister. But instead of relief at having regained his balance, he felt only dread. Dread of what he would see when he looked up. Dread of what might be descending the stairs to intercept him. Dread of whether he had lost all vestiges of sanity.

Upon glancing back up the cursed stairway though, his first two dreads were downgraded to morbid curiosity. Whatever he'd seen at the top of the stairs was gone. This only strengthened his third dread. He immediately wondered if sanity had completely forsaken him in a land where nightmares and reality existed side-by-side, neither one more or less tangible than the other.

Croome continued up the stairs at a measured pace. He was a practical man. He didn't believe in superstitions or fables. And he certainly didn't believe in ghosts, goblins and ghouls. It must have been something in his tea. He made a mental note to toss out the box and start a fresh one.

As he topped the stairs, he let out a slight laugh that sounded more like a snort. Surely it had been his imagination, because he was once again alone in the vacuous house with nary a sight nor sound of spectral demons.

Maybe it disappeared into my bedroom he reluctantly thought, but dismissed the idea at once, for he was certain it had been a fleeting vision and nothing more. However, he decided it couldn't hurt to exercise caution as he slowly and carefully opened the door to his sleeping quarters and cautiously peered through the narrow gap.

"HA!!" he said, plainly and clearly, as if he was some comic book character who existed in only two dimensions and spoke only in pixilated capital letters. But he felt less like a valiant super-hero character and more like a lily-livered lunatic who moistened his knickers when confronted by his own shadow.

As Croome proceeded through the doorway into his bedroom, he mumbled to himself. "My imagination and nothing m..." Croome practically jumped out of his trousers for suddenly he felt a tugging at his pant leg. His heart imploded, and he nearly cracked his head on the top doorframe. If he had any wits, he would certainly have been scared out of them.

Croome abruptly looked down toward what certainly must have been the devil's spawn intent upon dragging him deep down into the blazing depths of hell. What he saw was neither a demon nor a satanic spawn. It was indeed as black as night and as sinuous as a snake. But its eyes were curious rather than hideous and the sound that emanated from its throat was more comical than diabolical.

"Purrrrrrr?" Queried Black Magic, as if trying to ascertain Croome's level of sanity.

"Blast you, demon cat!!" Spat Croome as he reached down and lifted the charcoal feline in the crook of his arm. Magic was only slightly fazed and glanced at Croome with measured indifference. She was, after all, a cat; and cats were far above the silly flights of fantasy and fanaticism of preposterous people. She watched as Croome cautiously crept into his own bedroom looking left then right then suspiciously toward his bed as if he expected to see a corpse on top of it and serpents beneath.

After nearly bursting every artery in his chest, Croome was determined to put an end to these silly flights of fancy. No more pussyfooting around in his own house. It was time to exorcise his own ridiculous apparitions and regain some sensibility.

# Chapter 4 - A Spiritual Visit

Croome glanced cautiously about his somewhat cavernous and extremely outdated bedroom, much too large for one old man and his diminutive black pet. Next he strode into the adjoining bathroom, careful not to step on a cat that blended perfectly into the shadows.

Although unable to completely rid himself of the heebie-jeebies, he was now convinced that his demented delusions were nothing more than bad tea and too much talk of Halloween parties by his imbecilic son-in-law. Before retiring for the evening Croome picked up the solitary picture frame that adorned his bed-stand. As if enchanted by a magical spell, the stern scowl and years of frozen grimace melted from his face replaced by a look of pure love and adoration.

In his hands nestled a photo of the beautiful Patricia Croome, love of his life, denizen of his dreams.

"Happy birthday, darling. I bet you thought I'd forgotten." Croome slowly drew the framed photograph towards his lips, intending to plant a kiss upon the image of his dearly departed wife.

"THANKS YA OLD GROUCH!!"

Croome dropped the photo and was faintly aware of crashing glass as his heart raced back into the stratosphere. He quickly spun around fully expecting to see the spectral scarecrow. But instead he saw, floating in front of him, a shimmering face that he recognized immediately... the same face as in the picture frame that now lay shattered at his feet.

"P-P-Patricia??" Croome's voice bore the heavy burden of perplexity, nostalgia and complete terror, all at once. This same burden forced him back onto his bed as if he could no longer shoulder the heavy load that had been thrust upon him on this diabolically bewildering evening.

Croome began to tremble like an autumn leaf as the shimmering figure of his spectral spouse slowly advanced upon him filling him with hope and dread at the same time. He tried valiantly to comprehend what he was seeing and hearing. Croome was discovering that a stubborn disbelief in ghosts did not preclude their occasional visits.

The apparition descended upon Croome, covered him, nearly consumed him and in a voice that was both soothing and frightening whispered in his ear. "No it's not the tea."

If the recognizable face and familiar voice were not enough to convince Croome of his wife's presence, the clairvoyant comment left no doubt in his mind. Sweet Patricia always knew what he was thinking, usually a split second before he realized it himself.

"P-Patricia." Croome stammered, for a second time.

"P-positively p-precise." The hovering spirit replied with a haunting smile. "Remember the part in our wedding vows about …until death do we part?"

Croome could only weakly shake his head.

"Consider this a bonus round."

Despite his confusion and terror, Croome noticed the slinky shape of a familiar black cat twisting its glistening body around the legs of his spiritual wife who calmly reached down to pet the perplexed feline. For once in his life, Croome was not silent out of sullen cantankerousness but out of sheer bewilderment.

"What's the matter?" Plasmic Patricia continued stroking Black Magic with one hand while reaching up to her trembling husband with the other. A phantasmal finger faintly caressed Croome's upper lip. "Cat got your tongue?"

And now Decimus was certain that he was neither

dreaming nor hallucinating. The eyes may deceive and the ears may play tricks, but there is no fooling the heart. Croome recognized the humor and never forgot the playfulness. There was only one Patricia, and she was in the room with Croome.

"It is you!?! But it can't be you're..."

"Croaked? Dead? Deceased..."

"Pushing up daisies." Croome experimented with a smile, but a rather tentative one.

"Now that's the Decimus I remember. I seem to recall you had quite the sense of humor in our younger days." Patricia's spirit swirled around Croome much like the cat swirled around her ethereal legs. "But I understand you're a little bit out of practice?"

If the spirit of his deceased wife was not enough to perplex Croome, the conversation further frustrated his faculties. If he hadn't been a well-grounded man, he would have taken to babbling.

"You can't be here. You left long ago. There's no such thing as..."

"Ghosts?" That haunting smile. "There's no such thing as ghosts? Well, my dear, if you're having trouble with the concept of ghosts, then you're in for a very long evening."

Decimus Croome was not a man to lose control. He relished control, embraced control, lived for control. But there was only one person who had ever seen Decimus Croome when he wasn't in complete control. And above all, she had loved Decimus Croome, whether he was in control or out of control.

That person, that woman, that spirit was now floating around his... their bedroom. And Croome was completely unsure whether he liked it or not. Long repressed feelings were coming to the surface. Patricia was the love of his life. She was the only one who made him feel completely at ease. She knew him better than he knew himself.

But was this really Patricia who floated carefree above him, beneath him and around him? Was this not a ghost, a spirit, a specter? How did one both deeply love and morbidly fear something... someone at the same time? Come to think of it, he actually knew of some marriages that fit that description, but that was beside the point.

Croome closed his eyes, took a deep breath and then opened his eyes. He couldn't decide if this felt more like his first kiss or his first scary movie. "I have missed you more than you can imagine, Patricia. Where have you been and why have you returned?"

Again, that haunting laugh, but this time with an undertone of affection. "Where have I been?"

Patricia paused and floated directly in front of Decimus so that they were only inches apart. Rather than being ominous, her intimate proximity put him at ease. He wanted to reach out and touch her, kiss her, caress her. But he knew it would be futile. It would be like touching the breeze or caressing an illusion.

The shimmering spirit of Patricia seemed to share that feeling as she reached toward Decimus but was unable to actually touch him. Their eyes locked. "Where have I been?" She repeated. "Why, I have been with you my love. I have watched over you, walked beside you and felt your pain."

Croome pondered these words and couldn't decide if they were comforting or creepy. "Can you always see me? Have you been with me all this time?"

"I can always see your spirit."

"Then you know how much I have missed you. You know how much I need you and how miserable my life has been since you left?"

"Yes, Decimus. That is why I am here. I have seen you suffer, and I have seen those around you suffer right along with you." Patricia now hovered slightly above Croome, her hair floating weightlessly, her soft brown eyes filled with both compassion and disappointment.

"But Patricia, when you left it was like…"

"Decimus. Dear, sweet Decimus. I did not choose to leave you. You, more than anyone else, must know that I wanted to stay. I wanted to see our daughter grow to become a woman. I wanted to celebrate every Christmas, Thanksgiving and Halloween." Once again, she reached out as if to caress her beloved husband. "But most of all, I wanted to grow old with you, my darling."

"But if you didn't choose it, and I didn't choose it, then why? Why did I have to spend my life without the one I loved most? Why did our daughter have to grow up without her mother? Why…"

"You cannot choose when or how you die, but you can choose how you live." Patricia's eyes reflected the pain that Decimus had suffered and the love that he felt for her.

"That is why I have visited you tonight."

As if on cue, directed by some celestial choreographer, a single tear welled beneath the eye of each Croome, both the ethereal and corporeal. "Have you come to end my pain? Have you come to take me away with you?" Decimus pleaded, his single tear falling in unison with Patricia's.

"No my dear. It is not yet your time. For you still have many years in front of you."

A second tear followed by a third. "But I miss you so. Life has been..." Croome could not continue. He had not the words to express his feelings of sorrow for living without the love of his life.

"Life is what you make it, dear Decimus." And now Patricia resumed her swirling journey around her bewildered husband until her spirit engulfed him, her cheek next to his. Decimus could almost feel her warmth, smell her familiar aroma... But when he glanced in the same direction as his beloved, he was looking in a full-length mirror, the one he had gotten Patricia for their second wedding anniversary.

And he was all alone. There was no Patricia reflected in the mirror. For a moment he panicked.

"Don't worry dear." Her soft voice in his ear. "I'm still here with you..."

Decimus could see the faintly shining apparition of his wife beside him, around him.

"... but not for long." Now her voice seemed to be fading, the faint glow subsiding.

"Please don't leave!" Decimus pleaded.

"I must leave, my dear, just as you must stay. But please listen to what I have to tell you."

She continued. "I know you have been sad. You have been miserable. Everyone knows that. I know you have missed me, and I'm sorry for that."

"But I..."

The spirit of Patricia placed her long, slender, ghostly finger upon her husband's lips. "Hush dear Decimus. My time with you is limited, and what I have to say is important. You must heed my warning."

She continued, her voice growing softer with each syllable. "As I said, I have seen your struggles through these past years, and I have seen those around you suffer also. What has happened has happened. We cannot undo these things. All we can do is enjoy the time we have been given."

And now Patricia's wavering spirit once again faced Croome, but this time he had trouble discerning her features. What he did see was not as kindly and sweet. Her lovely grin seemed to be replaced by a more stern countenance.

"You have been neither enjoyed nor enjoyable, Decimus. In fact, you have been downright miserable... as a friend, as an employer, as a neighbor and as a father. Someday, we will be reunited, but today is not that day."

Patricia's spirit had almost completely faded. Her voice had also diminished noticeably. Soon she would be gone. "I will be leaving you now, Decimus. But you will not be alone this evening. At the stroke of midnight, in the earliest hours of Halloween, exactly thirty years after the birth of your only child, you will be visited by three spirits."

Croome could barely see a wisp of his wife. "Although that seems hauntingly appropriate, I don't th..."

"Goodbye, Decimus. Heed well the visions you are about to experience for they will reveal your life as it was, as it is and as it may yet be."

"These... these spirits. Will they tell me what I must

do...?"

"They will not tell you. They will show you. It is for you to decide..." As her voice disappeared, so too did her spirit.

Decimus reached out to emptiness. No tears this time, but excruciating loneliness. "Don't leave me Patricia. I cannot bear to lose you again. You were the one person who made me laugh... made me happy. I need you!"

A far off voice, "As many people need you Decimus."

"Happy birthday dear Patricia." Decimus Croome had been visited by the love of his life only to have her vanish once again leaving a silent room and a broken heart.

Croome lay back down on his bed. He thought about what Patricia had said. Three spirits would visit him. That was vaguely disturbing and more than just a little frightening, but for now he tried to bask in the afterglow of his recent visit from an angel. For truly Patricia was a heavenly guardian sent to lift his miserable spirits, if only for a short while.

Croome tried desperately to hang onto the vision of his sweet Patricia, but as the vision faded, so to did the warm glow until gradually, as if nothing had ever happened, the old Croome returned. "At the stroke of midnight, indeed.

Three spirits. Three Halloween spirits." Decimus almost laughed but found no room in his heart for cheer. "Pish posh." He whispered, feeling lonely, feeling forlorn but, above all, feeling overwhelmingly slumberous.

"Pish posh and poppycock." He whispered.

And with that, he faded off to sleep.

# Chapter 5 - The Spirit of Halloween Past

Croome awoke with a shiver and plucked a large, yellow-orange leaf off his chest. He wished that he had turned the thermostat up a little before going to bed. The penetrating cold and persistent breeze intensified the usual ache in his stiff, old body. Why was there a breeze in his bedroom and how did a leaf get into his house and onto his chest? He scanned the room then realized he had left his bedroom window wide open. The decades-old drapes, faded and a bit tattered, were wavering, like...

...like a ghost. Croome glanced quickly from side to side, hoping to see Patricia but dreading what else he might see. He was glad he was still fully dressed as he swung his legs over the side of the bed and ran his fingers through an unruly mop of hair.

But before he could rise, he sensed a presence in the room. He sat bolt upright, hesitantly scanned the room then looked back toward the swaying curtains. As the fog cleared from his head he realized he hadn't forgotten to close the window. How could he have forgotten to close it if he had never opened it in the first place? Why would he open the window on a freezing cold fall afternoon? That would be so wasteful, so inefficient, so unCroomelike.

But if he hadn't opened it, who had? Or *what* had?

He cautiously rose to his feet and crept stealthily toward the window with its fluttering drapes. The breeze caused another involuntary shiver that started at Croome's shoulders and traveled down his spine all the way to the tips of his toenails.

No sooner had the shuddering spasms subsided than Croome heard a noise that sent the shivers straight back up his spine and out the top of his head.

creak… creak

The noise, although slight at first, set off an alarm inside of Croome. Even before the noise he had detected something out of place in the room.

Creak… Creak

Something drew his attention away from the window and toward the far corner of the room.

CREAK… CREAK

There was definitely a presence that was every bit as palpable as the cold and the breeze.

**CREAK**

And that presence was sitting in the corner, opposite the bed, in a big wooden rocking chair.

creak… creak

It was, in fact, the very same chair that Croome normally used to remove his shoes each night before retiring to bed.

"Patricia?" Croome inquired hesitantly, hoping it was once again the spirit of his divinely departed darling.

***CREAK!!***

But it wasn't his dear, sweet Patricia. Whatever was in the chair, nestled deep within the shadows, was much bigger than Patricia's spirit had been. Much bigger and much more intimidating.

(The creaking stopped.)

A slight movement from the chair nearly sent Croome through the roof. Just when Croome began to wish the creepy creaking would resume, there came a very low and wicked-sounding rumble that quickly mutated into a diabolical laugh.

Or at least Croome assumed it was a laugh since, out of the deepest darkness of the far bedroom corner shone a wicked, glowing grin. It was a headless, bodiless, toothsome grin that grew in both size and intensity until it nearly blinded Croome.

Then the laughter stopped and the orange light dimmed. The grin seemed to be mutating into an evil frown. The rumbling subsided and was replaced with a black hole of silence that was followed by only one word.

"*Patricia?*"

The voice was gravelly, the tone mocking.

Then, whatever was in the chair leaned slowly and ominously forward. More appropriately, it glided forward, and Croome saw the color orange. But not a solid orange. More of a flickering orange like firelight shining through...

"Do I LOOK LIKE..." Suddenly the creature seemed to fly from the chair, into the light. It was hideous. Its head was a huge pumpkin or, more appropriately a jack-o-lantern. "... PATRICIA..." It flew toward Croome first soaring toward the ceiling then dive-bombing, like a wicked kamikaze, directly toward him. "...TO YOU?!!!!?"

Croome made an awkward and desperate flop back toward his bed...

... and missed.

Wicked laughter shook the room with an ominous tone that was intertwined with humor like the derisive laughter of a schoolyard bully who enjoys the terror and suffering he inflicts upon his helpless victims. Croome tightly closed his eyes and awaited the final deadly onslaught. But the onslaught never came.

Instead there was only silence. Dead, suffocating silence filled the room with its vacuous presence. Croome cautiously cracked open one eye to a thin slit, barely enough to see a distorted but empty room in front of him. He never once thought he was dreaming. None of this was a dream or even a nightmare. It was unbelievable, inconceivable and yet as real as his relentlessly hammering heart.

Croome cracked his other eye to a paper-thin slit. Still nothing. Gradually, he opened both eyes but refused to look around for fear of what he might see. And indeed he saw nothing directly in front of him; but he knew he was not alone. His bedroom had become hell, and Satan was his new roommate.

Still looking straight ahead, Croome elbowed up to a sitting position, wincing in pain from the bruises of his recent fall. He had trouble standing up without turning his head one way or the other. He was like a young child who believed that, as long as he couldn't see the boogeyman, the boogeyman didn't exist.

As soon as he was fully standing, Croome took a deep breath and braced himself to look around the room. He didn't try to delude himself. He knew the creature was still there. He could feel its presence even without seeing it. Faintly he heard a rustling noise growing nearer to him. Then without warning he felt it. Something hideously hairy brushed against his leg.

Instinctively he kicked out, trying to punt the unseen terror away from him. He immediately regretted it when his foot made contact with something squishy and furry like a giant, hairy spider. Then he heard a pitiful howling sound and saw something black flailing through the air toward the window.

He was tempted to close his eyes again and block out the sight of the demon. Whatever it was would now be vengeful as well as hideous. But he knew that shutting his eyes would do no good, so he grit his teeth and glanced toward the black creature seemingly suspended in midair writing and snarling near the window.

It was much smaller than he expected. Smaller and strangely familiar. In fact it looked just like...

"Magic?" The indignant black cat was clinging to the drapes and glaring furiously at Croome.

If Croome wasn't still so afraid of the evil that lurked nearby, he would have breathed a sigh of relief, maybe even enjoyed a brief chuckle. But he was currently in even less of a chuckling mood than normal; and he was never much of a chuckler.

The force of the unintended punt had sent the cat flying directly toward the open window. Fortunately, the old tattered curtains had provided a secure claw-hold for the terrified animal and saved him from flying out of the opening and all the way down to the ground below where she may or may not have landed on her feet and may or may not have used up one of her nine lives. Croome took one tentative step toward the window to help the pitifully suspended cat regain its rightful position in the house, if not its dignity.

But one step was all that Croome got when suddenly and surprisingly he was verbally accosted by the demon pumpkin head again as it roared, "WHO? WHO? WHO?" This time the cursed laughter was followed by a singsong chorus, "WHO LET THE CATS OUT?"

Now the laughter was playful yet mocking. And the orange gourd head was instantly in Croome's face again, pointing a viney finger right at him. "YOU! YOU! YOU! YOU!"

Croome backed away from the creature until he could back no further and plopped down on the bed, his eyes nearly as big as his rounded mouth that was wailing one word and one word only.

"NOOOOOOOOOOOOOO!!!!"

The pumpkin-headed beast tilted its gigantic head back in laughter, only this time the laughter was silent. Croome was worried that he had lost not only his mind but his ability to hear as well. But he didn't worry for long.

"YYYYYYESSSSSSSS!!" Wailed the creature, now clearly mocking Croome.

The sudden mockative ghostly outburst was followed by another moment of silence followed by the angry hissing and sputtering of Black Magic as she indignantly clawed her way down from the drapes and plopped herself angrily onto the floor while casting one evil eye in Croome's direction and the other wary eye in the direction of their raucous visitor.

"THAT IS ONE ANGRY CAT." The spirit barked out in the gravelly voice of an old vaudeville performer.

Decimus realized that he was witnessing one of the three spirits Patricia had warned him about. His fear was gradually being replaced by irritation. It would have been nice if she had warned him about this particular spirit's bedside manners.

"Ar-ar-are you one of the spirits I was warned would...."

With that, the spirit once again flew directly toward the ceiling then dove headlong back down at Croome. As it was about to crash into him, it abruptly stopped and vomited a slimy, orange mixture of pumpkin seeds and guts. Upon expelling its ooey, gooey, malodorous mess directly onto Croome's face, it stuck its putrid, pumpkin pie-hole barely inches from Croome's nose and bellowed, "YOUR MOTHER SUC...""

It's jack--o-lantern head spun 360 degrees around to face him again.

"...CESSFULLY RAISED AN IDIOT!!!"

Croome tentatively reached up and wiped the slimy, soggy, seeds from his face. He was glad to see the spirit had floated backward a few feet and was now less terrified yet more disgusted by the unwelcome guest.

"Good gads ghost, you scared the Dickens out of me. Who are you? Why are you here? What do you want of me?" Croome's voice was still a bit unsteady but he tried hard to maintain control, hoping not to sound like a frightened child.

"My, my… lots of questions. Let's start with who am I." The Spirit began morphing from his pumpkinous shape to an amorphous floating specter complete with a flowing white body and round, dark holes for a mouth, nose and eyes. "I am a ghost!!!" He flew around Croome in a corkscrew motion and began wailing. "Booooooooo!!!"

When he got up to Croome's head, he whispered in his ear. "By the way, I've known lots of ghosts in my days, and none of them ever say Booooo. I'm not sure what's up with that?"

In a flash, the Spirit converted back to his original orange pumpkin self only he was now just one massive hovering head with sharp fang-like teeth and fiery glistening eyes that looked as if they were windows into the deepest bowels of purgatory. "I am an evil Jack-o-lantern who has come to haunt your every waking moment!!"

Croome stepped backward and closed his eyes, positive the possessed pumpkin was going to swallow him whole. But when he heard nothing more from his vial visitor, he dared to open his eyes and was relieved to see the original Spirit was back.

But he wasn't relieved for long; suddenly the Spirit began flying round and around him, moving faster and faster causing a horrible tornado of putrid air to lift Croome off the ground and spin him into what seemed like a whirlpool of doom. Everything was a blur except the pumpkin face that kept rotating around his head and bellowing, "I am the Spirit of Halloween Past." And when the spinning got so bad that Croome was about to lose the meager contents of his stomach, it stopped even quicker than it started, dropping the nauseated old man onto his boney keister on the floor.

Long after Croome stopped spinning, the room continued going round and round. As soon as he began to regain his senses and some small sense of stability, his gruesome guest stuck out a bleach-boned hand and said, "But you can call me Pepo. Nice to meet you."

Croome had absolutely no idea what to do, so he just sat on the floor and waited for the room to stop twirling.

"As for why I'm here…" The spirit was no longer lurking in the shadows, changing shapes nor flying around maniacally. He enthusiastically shook Croome's limp hand and spoke in a conspiratorial tone. "I've come to take you on a little trip."

Croome was able to get a better look at the marauding menace and realized there was actually some type of body under the giant, orange head. Or rather there was a long, shimmering robe of black and silver that appeared to sway mysteriously to and fro, with a constant fluid movement that reminded Croome of a cobra preparing to pounce.

"A little trip down memory lane." The spirit's brittle voice had grown quieter and sounded less like a foghorn and more like autumn leaves rattling through the bare boned branches of a dark and forlorn tree.

It was then that Croome realized why the spirit's robe seemed to be in constant motion. What had appeared to be silver threads were actually intertwining cobwebs, and the movement came from hundreds, maybe even thousands of spiders of various sizes, crawling in, around and through the webbing.

The Spirit drifted toward Croome and extended a long, skeletal appendage from under its shimmering robe. Croome was compelled to retreat but stood his ground knowing that resistance was futile. The spirit had grown close enough that Croome could examine all its sordid details with horrifying clarity. He observed the long, boney fingers that were now extended to him.

"What is it you want from me?" Croome implored, knowing full well what the spirit wanted.

"My, my, we're just full of questions." Eerily, the Spirit's voice changed in mid-sentence and sounded exactly like Croome's own voice. "Do you know what happened to Socrates when he asked too many questions?"

Croome couldn't help but wonder how much the Spirit knew about his past misdeeds, but he didn't have time to ponder as he noticed that Black Magic had overcome his indignity and was now batting at one of the spiders dangling from the spirit's robe. Suddenly, like a kernel of popcorn bursting from its shell, the spider tripled in size and batted back at the mischievous cat whose eyes nearly bugged out of his head with astonishment.

Normally Croome would have been amused by Magic's sudden surprised look but, with a boney protuberance pointing directly at him, Croome was not in the mood for humorous feline antics.

Croome knew what was expected of him, and he had no choice. So with extreme reluctance, he reached out and grasped the fingers that felt like brittle branches from a withered old oak tree.

"Where are we going, Spirit?" Croome enquired, fearful of the answer yet filled with morbid curiosity.

"We are going to visit the haunts of your past, Decimus Croome." The spirit sounded less like a frightening ghoul and more like a wise but cantankerous old professor.

# Chapter 6 - Memory Lane

"It's dark out." Croome bemoaned, "And cold."

Bemoaning got him nowhere, so Croome attempted pleading. "I am not prepared for any kind of journey on a night such as this." The spirit drifted toward the window and Croome's voice went from pleading to terrified. "Where are we going spirit?" Croome tried pulling away as they neared the second floor window.

It appeared as if they were heading right for the edge of a twenty-foot drop off. Even in his spry days of youthful immortality, such a fall would have injured Croome. As a frail old man it would certainly mean serious injury or possibly even...

Croome tried desperately not to think about it as he continued his hopeless struggle right up to the ledge of the open window. As they approached the precipitous drop, Croome squeezed his eyelids shut and stifled the urge to cry out. But at the last minute the spirit rose into the air along with a very frightened and quivering Croome.

They began to drift effortlessly, as if they were as light as fallen leaves soaring on the autumn breeze. Croome let out a pathetic, involuntary whimper as they flew out the window and into the night sky. The last thing he saw, as he looked back, was his pesky black cat, Magic, peering out the window in astonishment at two floating apparitions slowly disappearing above the forest.

Croome summoned the courage to pry open his eyes, first into micro-thin cracks, then slowly all the way until he could see his surroundings. "You have told me we are visiting my past." Croome's voice wavered, then his body shivered from both the cold and fright. "But where and..."

Croome was about to ask what particular part of his past when, through the mists of both time and fog, he saw a distinctly recognizable sight. The closer they got, the greater the feeling of recognition and nostalgia. For directly below them was a familiar schoolhouse. It was not just any school but Croome's childhood alma mater. Although he had never seen it from this birds-eye view, Croome identified it instantly, and it deluged him with a flood of memories.

It was the school where he had not only learned to read and write but where he made friends, played games and received his first innocent kiss. It was where he had spent a good part of his boyhood, in the classrooms, on the playground and in the surrounding woodlands.

Suddenly Croome's ghostly guide swooped downward as if dive-bombing the school. They dropped so precipitously Croome feared they were going to crash into the elementary enclave; at the last moment the pumpkin pilot changed course and flew directly alongside the building, close enough to peer into the windows. Croome could see the empty desks, book-lined shelves and quaint old chalkboards.

The second classroom they passed was more difficult to view as its windows were cluttered with rectangles of paper hanging over nearly every square inch. At first the papers appeared to contain hieroglyphic scribbling from some long-lost pagan culture. But upon further investigation, they turned out to be priceless artwork that filled Croome with joy. This particular artwork contained barnstorming bats, flying witches, wide-eyed owls, haunted houses, tattered scarecrows and colorful autumn leaves pressed ever so carefully between sheets of waxed paper.

Croome wanted to stop and examine each priceless masterpiece. He had not seen such joyfully garish displays of Halloween art since his childhood. He briefly wondered why he couldn't remember seeing any such conspicuous exhibitions in his daughter's classroom. Was it because such Halloween traditions were no longer practiced or because he had spent so little time at his daughter's school... in her life?

Before he had time to figure out the correct answer, he noticed the schoolhouse was rapidly receding from view. He shot one last wistful glance back before realizing they were briskly approaching a familiar forest from his childhood. It was a small wooded patch of wilderness that separated the schoolyard from his own neighborhood.

Even before they entered the forest, Croome detected the pine-scented odors of his youthful stomping grounds where he had spent endless hours exploring woodland trails, building tree forts and playing hide-and-seek among the evergreens. Below their feet, as they deftly navigated the forested maze, Croome spotted brief glimpses of babbling brooks, shimmering ponds and meandering footpaths. All these sites reminded him of a carefree childhood spent outdoors from sunup to sundown, playing, exploring and enjoying endless merriment.

Croome expected, at any moment, to emerge from the forest into the backyard of his childhood home. But the spirit took an unexpected turn and, when the pair emerged from the forest, they ended up on the town's bucolic Main Street. First they saw the modest homes of those who lived in the quaint old town. Then the houses gave way to equally modest business buildings as it began to darken and the streetlights winked on, one after another.

Croome's face lit up with joy as he saw his favorite business in the town - Croome's Hardware. His smile broadened as he observed the tail-finned cars and snub-nosed pickup trucks parked directly in front of the store as well as a sparse gaggle of people walking the streets.

The ghost veered to the left and flew directly into the open door of the hardware store where he lit ever-so-gently in front of Croome's most cherished sight yet. For standing in front of him, no more than three feet away, was the congenial, industrious and very-much-alive Stanley Croome.

It had been so long since Croome had seen his father. The old man didn't look old at all, but splendidly robust and vigorous. And who should be standing beside him, standing no more than four feet tall from the bottoms of his worn sneakers to the tippy-top of his comically cow-licked hair? Of course it was a very young Decimus Croome himself.

"Recognize anyone?" Asked the spirit as he looked back and forth between old Decimus and young Dessy.

Croome just smiled as he absorbed every detail of the nostalgic scene being played out like reruns from an old television show.

The Ghost of Halloween Past tapped the smiling Decimus Croome on the shoulder and pointed toward the three people in Croome's Hardware store.

It was then that Croome realized, it wasn't a customer they were talking to but old Jake Talmidge, the man who had worked with his father for so many years in days gone by. Once again though, he looked younger than when Decimus had last seen him.

A lifetime of memories flew back to Decimus Croome as he watched these scenes from his own childhood. Jake Talmidge had a son about young Dessy's age and they were pals in elementary school.

Croome could now hear his father talking to Talmidge,

his lifelong friend and store employee. "Isn't it about time you found your way home Jake?" The elder Croome asked. "I believe you have some young ones who will want to be trick-or-treating soon."

Jake reached out and tussled young Dessy's mop of hair. "What about this young fellow, Stan? I don't suppose he'll be interested in trick-or-treating this year?" He knew full well the answer but enjoyed teasing young Decimus.

"Oh, I don't think there's any force on earth that could keep Dessy and Tessa from trick-or-treating. But I think Maggie can handle the Halloween duties just fine this year."

Once again, Decimus smiled to think of his mother, Margaret Croome, and sister, Tessa. He knew his dad was right. Nothing kept them from making their Halloween rounds. He remembered one year when they had gone out trick-or-treating in an October blizzard, despite their mother's fussing and fretting.

Jake Talmidge removed his work apron, folded it neatly and placed it on a shelf behind the front checkout counter of the store. He took one last opportunity to rumple young Dessy's hair. "Are you sure you can run this place without me for the next couple hours?" He directed his question at his boss, Stan Croome.

"I don't imagine we'll be getting many customers on Halloween night, Jake. Now you head on home and tell your kids to stop by our house. I'll bet Maggie'll have an extra treat or two for 'em." Stan Croome was now sweeping the already immaculate floor of Croome's Hardware Store, more out of habit than need.

Just before exiting the store, Jake turned toward Dessy. "It must be about time for you to head home young man, before all your neighbors run out of candy." With that, the jovial Talmidge whisked out the door and home to his children.

Evidently the pumpkin-headed Spirit had shown Croome what he intended, so he held out a grizzled and boney hand. Croome reluctantly grasped one of the extended limbs, and they rose slowly into the air. He heard the younger Decimus asking his father, "Why don't we sell Halloween decorations in our store, Papa?"

His dad laughed that warm and hearty laugh Croome had missed all these years. "Whoever heard of Halloween decorations in a hardware store? You have such an enormous imagination, for such a little guy. Maybe, when you are running the store someday, you can sell all the holiday decorations you'd like. But for now, young man, it is time for you to go home and become the scariest trick-or-treater in the entire town"

Just before soaring out of the store, old Croome heard his younger self asking his father one last question. "Why can't you come trick-or-treating with us, Dad?"

They were once again flying through the town. Croome remembered the answer to his question of so many years past. His father knew that Decimus's mother would do a wonderful job preparing the children for their trick-or-treating foray. But he felt it was important to let Mr. Talmidge, who had recently lost his wife, go home and spend time with his own children on Halloween. Croome remembered his father as one who always concerned himself with the well being of others as well as the needs of his own family. As these memories raced through Croome's mind, he couldn't help but reflect on how he treated his own employee, Sam Bobbich.

Before he had time for much reflection, Croome recognized the neighborhood they were entering. It was the neighborhood of his youth, and he fondly recalled each house and the people who lived within them. He could tick off not only the owners but also their children and most of their pets.

However, fondest of all, he remembered his own childhood home, and he felt a warm knot in his stomach as they approached that hallowed domicile. Aaah the games he had played in that yard. Endless afternoons of red rover in the spring, sandlot football in the summer, hide-and-seek in the fall and snowball fights in the winter. What comfort he felt as they flew down the chimney and into the family living room where he heard two fondly familiar voices that flooded his heart with joy.

The voices belonged to a couple of the most beautiful young ladies Croome had seen in a long time. His sister, Tessa, and his mother, both seeming young and feisty, were squabbling rather heatedly. His sister, wearing a rather provocative outfit, was showing off a bit more flesh than their mother would tolerate.

"But this is the costume all my friends will be wearing." Tessa said, dressed in a wardrobe she had no doubt seen on television or in the latest teen magazine. She was garbed in a multi-colored top that didn't quite reach all the way down to the waistline of an incredibly skin-tight pair of pants that looked as if they were threatening to burst into shreds at any moment. Her shoes looked like they could also double as circus clown stilts with heels that would have been comical if they didn't look so uncomfortable. Croome had no idea where she might have gotten such clothing, not to mention the sparkling jewelry and conspicuous make-up, but he couldn't help but smile at both the costume and the conversation it inspired.

"I don't care if the Queen of England is wearing this outfit! It's not what you'll be wearing tonight or any other night as long as you live under this roof!! Now get upstairs and change into something more appropriate!!!" She swiveled toward the front door as she heard the knob rattle and felt a gust of cool autumn air. Then she quickly turned back to her daughter who was stomping up the stairs. "And make sure you put on something warm! It's winter out there, young lady!!"

"Technically it's not winter for another month and a half." Tessa growled over her shoulder as she stomped up the stairs.

Despite the altercation, Maggie Croome was wearing a

contented smile and turned back to the front door. "You take off your shoes Dessy," In the Croome household, Margaret was Maggie and Decimus was Dessy. "Then if you have any intention of going trick-or-treating tonight, you'd better find your way to the kitchen so we can get you into your costume. And you'd better make it fast because you're not staying out past 9:00 and it's nearly dark outside already."

At the door, young Dessy Croome quickly pried off his shoes, neglecting to untie them as usual. "We've got plenty of time, Mom. My friends won't be here until 6:30."

"We **don't** have PLENTY OF TIME!!" His mom reverted back to the same agitated-parent voice she had been using with Tessa just a couple minutes earlier. "We still have to get some warm food in you and get you decorated for Halloween."

"You don't decorate people." Decimus corrected his mother. "You decorate cakes and houses. And why do I have to eat? We'll have plenty of candy to eat for the next week."

"*That's* why you have to eat. This may be the last healthy meal you'll have for days. Now get in the kitchen. TESSA!!

GET DOWN HERE AND EAT DINNER WITH YOUR BROTHER!!!"

This was the Croome household that Decimus remembered. A home filled with activity, bantering and joy. A household of work, play and love.

As old Croome gazed around at his childhood home, he could hear his younger self, in the kitchen. "I don't want to be a hobo. I don't even know what a hobo is."

Old Decimus followed the Halloween Spirit into the kitchen and saw his mother liberally applying petroleum jelly to young Dessy's face. "A hobo is what you'll be if you don't start getting better grades in school. Now quit squirming so much." She artfully dabbed coffee grounds onto the sticky ointment that covered his jaw.

Dessy looked up when he heard his sister stamping around upstairs, and his mother let out an exasperated groan. "I said quit squirming around. Do you want your beard to cover your whole face?"

Dessy grinned. "Cool. Then I can be a werewolf instead of a stupid hobo." Then his grin turned into a grimace. "Yuck. How do you guys drink coffee? It smells disgusting." The younger Croome continued to squirm and struggle under his mom's patient hands. "Why can't I just be a superhero like everyone else?"

Just then Tessa walked into the kitchen appropriately attired in a warm coat and long pants. "You look more like a midget Fred Flintstone than a hobo." She said to her brother as she started putting dishes and silverware on the table.

"Very funny," young Dessy whined. "Why aren't you wearing a Halloween costume?"

"Because Mom wants me to dress like some dorky princess or something. So I'm not going to dress up this year." Tessa glanced in her mom's direction as if trying to gauge her mood.

"Suit yourself, little Miss Priss. We'll see how much candy you get without a costume. You know the neighborhood rule: no costume, no candy." Mrs. Croome put the finishing touches on Dessy and retrieved a pot of soup from the stove. "Remember, this is your last year of trick-or-treating. Once you're a teenager, you aren't allowed to trick-or-treat anymore."

"Oh fudge knuckles." Tessa said, looking away from her mother. "There sure are a lot of stupid rules in this town."

"Don't you talk like that young lady!" Tessa's mom stopped grooming her son long enough to shoot an exasperated glare at her daughter.

Young Dessy started chanting, "Fudge knuckles, fudge knuckles..." having absolutely no idea what a fudge knuckle was but loving the sound of it.

"Now look what you started." Mrs. Croome shot one last glare at her daughter before deciding to move on. "Besides, I don't think those are really rules as much as they are guidelines. And I don't think they're just in this town."

Croome got the impression that his mother hadn't been a big fan of the "guidelines" either, but she didn't share these opinions aloud. The kids quickly gobbled down their soup, then Mrs. Croome reapplied coffee grounds to replace the ones Dessy messed up while eating.

"Gross. Coffee grounds taste even worse than they smell." Young Dessy made a disgusting face. "We should have eaten BEFORE we put on these grotesque coffee whiskers."

"I'll remember that next time you're a hobo." His mom's subtle sarcasm flew right over her son's head.

A knock at the front door signaled the arrival of the

neighborhood tribe. Maggie smiled to see only one superhero at the door and a whole herd of homemade costumes similar to the hobo outfit Dessy was wearing. Behind the young boys was a smaller group of young girls about Tessa's age. Just like Tessa, none of them was wearing a costume.

The two Croome kids slithered around their mother and joined their friends. The girls immediately started complaining with one voice. "My mom wanted me to wear..."

"Have a nice Halloween kids!" Mrs. Croome chanted, receiving evil glares from the teenage girls. "Be home **BY** 9:00. And you older kids stay with the younger ones."

The two groups of trick-or-treaters started moving away from the house, seemingly oblivious to the shouts of Maggie Croome who was still relaying instructions. "And don't eat any unwrapped candy."

As soon as they were away from the watchful eyes of parents, the girls ditched their boring coats and baggy pants to reveal their original bedazzling costumes underneath. They weren't even fazed when their younger siblings started the inevitable chorus of "I'm telling mom that you're wearing that ugly costume."

One of the older girls offered the first bribe. "You can have half my candy if you shut your ugly little mouth."

The negotiations continued. "All your candy or you're in trouble."

The deal was struck, and the groups parted ways, neither wanting to be burdened by the other.

Old Croome enjoyed watching the young hobgoblins almost as much as they enjoyed their trick-or-treating forays. The neighborhood adults who were generously doling out handfuls of candy also seemed to be relishing the whole masquerade and, in addition to candy, showered the youngsters with praise and questions about their costumes.

"Oh to be young again and have free reign of the neighborhood. Everyone seems to be having such fun. Whatever happened to those innocent times of fun and friends, costumes and candy?" Old Decimus Croome questioned his guiding spirit.

"Fun indeed." Now that the Spirit knew Decimus' nickname, he couldn't resist one last dig. "That is a very good point, Dessy. Maybe you would be the best one to answer that question."

Croome wasn't the least bit hesitant to share his point of view. "People have just grown so crotchety and..."

The Spirit interrupted Croome. "Really. Now who do you know that is crotchety?"

Croome never was a big fan of the big-toothed grins that adorned Jack-o-lantern faces, and he was even less appreciative of the smug grin that dominated the orange face of his melodramatic tour guide. "Is this why we are here? Is this why we have visited this time and place, Spirit? Are you trying to show me the error of my ways?" Croome sounded half irritated and half remorseful.

The Spirit ignored Croome's question and sounded like a Twilight Zone narrator when he announced, "It would appear that we have seen all we need to see here. Let us continue our little journey through time and space."

Croome cast one last reflective glance at the carefree trick-or-treaters, then hesitantly reached for the Spirit's sleeve, abruptly jerking back at the sight of one particularly agitated arachnid dangling from his escort's shimmering garment. "I have no choice but to follow where you lead!! But couldn't we stay here just a bit longer?"

"What is it that you would see here? Is not all this Halloween nonsense just a waste of time? Are not these Halloween revelers just so much sentimental absurdity?"

Croome recognized his own words with some regret. "It is only that I wish to see more of this joyful chapter in my life."

"Joyful? For what reasons do you find it joyful?" The Spirit inquired, but did not wait for an answer as he soared skyward with Croome in tow. "My time with you is limited, and we have much to see."

# Chapter 7: The Best of Times

Croome hung on for all he was worth as the resolute Spirit swept him up and purposefully whisked him away to an obscure destination in a bygone era. The two wayfaring time travelers whooshed upward and onward into the chilly autumn air and were soon beholding a Halloween scene that was noticeably different than the previous one. For one thing, the Halloween revelers appeared to be much older than the young trick-or-treaters in their last destination. Most of the costume-clad partiers were unfamiliar to Croome.

But one in particular caught his eye. She was a sight to behold in a costume that made his sister's look positively innocent. Croome felt a sensation that he had long since forgotten when suddenly he realized whom the stunning creature was.

"Patricia," he gasped. "It is Patricia, and she looks every bit as beautiful as when I first met her so many..."

"There is a very good reason for that, Decimus." The Spirit intoned, and then watched the look on Croome's face as he realized the historic moment he was witnessing.

Old Croome stared in fascination as a young man approached Patricia. He was dressed as a knight in shining armor. Croome watched as the handsome young knight summoned up his chivalric courage to speak with the fair maiden.

"I have come to rescue a sweet damsel in distress." He said, taking one knee and lightly kissing her hand.

She coyly retrieved her hand and took a small step backward, looking the errant knight directly in his ne'er-do-well eyes. "I don't believe I was in distress until you showed up."

Cool and calm on the outside, stomach churning on the inside, the knight carried on. "Oh how wrong you are, my sweet lady. For many dragons have been eying you on this All Hallows Evening. They come in many shapes and sizes, but each one has the same sinister plans for you my dear."

"And your plans are less sinister?" She eyed him with a heavy dose of skepticism and a smidgen of interest.

"I assure you fair lady, my plans are nothing but noble and righteous." With that, the silver-tongued knight retrieved the withdrawn hand and planted a chivalrous kiss on the backside.

Croome watched it all from above with growing fascination and remembered that Patricia didn't withdraw her hand a second time. "This is the night we first met. It was a Halloween party." But then he saw a castle-shaped birthday cake on a rickety old table near the smitten young couple. "No, it was a birthday party. It was both a Halloween party and birthday party for Patricia. Her birthday was on the day before Halloween. All-Hallows-Eve."

Then Croome let out a small gasp as he remembered she had told him that her real first name was not Patricia, but Eve. Eve Patricia Corning. That was when he realized that he was falling in love. It was such a small revelation, but he felt as if she had shared a sacred trust with him. She had shared a small part of her life with him.

Croome cast a furtive glance back at the Spirit then resumed his narrative. "This was the very first night we'd ever met. I had gone away to college and came back home for the weekend. Some of my old high school buddies insisted that I join them at this party; they said I had to dress like a knight in shining armor. They wouldn't tell me why. They said I would know when I got there."

Croome wiped at some excess moisture that had inconveniently collected on his bottom eyelid. "And they were right. As soon as I saw her, I knew that she was meant to be my princess. I knew that I wanted to spend the rest of my life with her from that very first evening."

"You were quite the smooth-talking lady's man." The Spirit commented.

"No." Croome was mesmerized by the scene below him and was barely aware of the ghostly presence beside him. "No. I wasn't normally much of a smooth talker. But something about Patricia just gave me confidence. From the very start, she lifted my spirits. It's almost as if she turned me from a paltry peasant into a noble knight."

"Like I said..." The spirit reached out to Decimus.

Croome looked forlornly from the Spirit to the scene below him and back to the Spirit. "Please. Can we stay just a bit longer?" Croome was not in the habit of begging and had absolutely no experience with groveling; but he was willing to try anything for just a few more minutes with his precious Patricia. "These were the happiest moments of my life. All I ask is for a few more minutes, Spirit."

The Spirit also looked back and forth between Croome

and the scene below. Then, in truly compassionate and romantic form he rendered his verdict. "Blah, blah, blah." Without delay, Croome was spirited away. Evidently the Spirit was unfazed by Decimus's transformation. "Are you sure it was the happiest moment?" The spirit nudged Croome who was craning his neck to look back toward his precious Patricia.

Before Croome could answer, he noticed numerous changes in the scene beneath them. They no longer appeared to be in a home but were now in some type of restaurant. And it wasn't just any restaurant. Croome realized that the men were dressed in dark suits while the female diners wore evening dresses.

Each table had a fall-themed centerpiece with flickering candles providing a romantic atmosphere. It was still obviously around Halloween time. The decorations on the walls were unmistakably Octoberish. Many things were the same, in fact. There was a similar castle birthday cake and the dashing young Croome was even still in the same knightly outfit, albeit a little tighter fit over a slightly more mature Croome.

But Patricia was not in her princess outfit and she

seemed a bit confused by the cake and shining armor. "You didn't tell me we were supposed to be dressed up for Halloween." Her face was truly a portrait of puzzlement.

Then she looked around at all the primly dressed people staring at them. She leaned toward her shining knight and whispered. "I think you may be a bit overdressed." Her tone was somewhere between embarrassed and playful.

Once again, young Decimus reached out for Patricia's hand. "I didn't want to spoil the surprise. And I don't care how I'm dressed or what these knaves think of my dazzling armor." With an uncharacteristically dramatic flourish, he swept his plastic sword around the room. "For I only care about one thing my lady."

With that, he took off one of his knightly gloves and held out a ring to his wide-eyed maiden. "And that one thing is you."

There was a smattering of oohs and aahs from the (mostly female) patrons of the restaurant and even a small round of applause, but young Decimus seemed unaware as he gazed into Patricia's eyes. "I am not able to provide you with a castle." He said, pointing with his sword toward the castle-cake. "I may not even be able to wear this shining outfit every day of our lives."

With that, he awkwardly lowered himself to one knee. "But one thing I do want every day, for the rest of our lives, is to spend them with you."

More muffled mutterings from the surrounding tables.

"Eve Patricia Corning, will you marry me?"

The tears on old Croome's cheeks fell in synchrony with those of young Patricia. By this point, there was a full-on standing ovation from throughout the restaurant galley as both diners and employees cheered for the newly engaged couple.

Now it was the Spirit's turn to lean toward a much older Decimus Croome and whisper in his ear. "So do you still think that our previous stop at the birthday party was the happiest moment of your life?"

"Maybe not." Croome removed the glisten from his eyes. "No this was definitely..."

"Aah aah aah!!" The spirit interrupted. "Not so fast, my mortal friend."

And suddenly they were transported to yet another room. Only this one was much more subdued, much quieter, but no less joyous. Young Croome was no longer holding a glistening plastic sword, but his smile glistened every bit as bright. In place of the weapon, he was holding a young Croome progeny. Or progenette, to be precise.

He gazed down onto the most innocent and adorable face he had ever seen.

"Is she asleep yet?" A slightly older but no less beautiful Patricia asked the proud young father.

"Yes. She's sound asleep. Should I wake her up?" The glowing young Croome asked.

The abrasive Spirit let out a snort. "Let's see if he's still eager to wake her up in a couple weeks."

Croome ignored his unsentimental travel partner and proudly recalled his daughter's birth. "She was born on her mother's birthday, so we had another Eve in the family. Isn't she beautiful?"

"You've seen one baby, you've seen them all." The Spirit tried to maintain his cantankerous façade; however even he couldn't help but smile at the wriggling little bundle of joy in the arms of Daddy Decimus.

————————————————

One thing seemed to be the same in every room they visited. Halloween decorations adorned the walls. Even the mobile over the crib was a menagerie of Halloween critters spinning around to the beat of "Werewolves of London."

"Now what is that quaint little phrase of yours whenever someone wishes you a happy Halloween?" The Spirit enquired.

At first Croome shot the Spirit a perplexed look. Then he made the connection and muttered an inaudible answer.

"I'm sorry, but I couldn't hear you." The Spirit looked down at his shimmering robe. "How about you guys? Could you hear him?"

All the spiders shook their head in unison, a gesture that would have been cute… if they weren't spiders.

"I said '*pish posh and poppycock.*'" Croome muttered, just a bit louder.

"Seems like an awfully negative thing to say for someone who had so many memorable Halloweens." This time all the spiders nodded in the affirmative. "And it seemed like most of those memories were pretty darned positive."

"Yes." Croome hesitated, his face turning from radiant

to somber.

"Most of them were wonderful," His face continued the transformation from somber to forlorn. "But not all of them."

# Chapter 8 - The Worst of Times

"Yeah. About that…" The Spirit had somehow mysteriously donned a ragged old cowboy hat and spoke with an exaggerated western drawl. "We have one last stop before I mosey on back to the ol' pumpkin patch."

Suddenly they were in what appeared to be a very different room. Or at least the atmosphere was quite different. Actually the room was the same one as before and, as they entered it, they saw Decimus, visibly older and exponentially less joyful. He was bent over his beautiful Patricia who was looking neither beautiful nor comfortable. She was part-lying and part-sitting on a folding bed that had been set up in the living room. She had tubes in her arm, tubes in her nose and even more tubes coming out from under the hospital gown she was wearing.

This, however, was not the jovial, smiling, joyful Patricia of the past three visits. This Patricia was obviously in pain and fighting bravely not to show it. An exceedingly downcast looking young Decimus stood by her side, holding tight to her hand, feeding her the love and courage that no tube or modern miracle medical machine could ever provide.

"Are you sure you don't want to be in the hospital, sweetheart?" Now young Croome's voice wavered as he gently squeezed Patricia's pale hands in his own trembling grasp.

Patricia's voice was strained and distant. "There is nothing more they can do for me in the hospital, Dessy." She slowly and painfully turned her head in the direction of a third person that was standing on the other side of the bed from her struggling husband.

A man that old Decimus immediately recognized as Patricia's doctor ran both of his hands through his hair, obviously trying to find the right words. "I'm afraid she's right. I wish it was otherwise, Decimus." Croome remembered this man almost as if he was a family member. He had been so kind to Patricia and so empathetic. In fact, Croome sometimes wondered how this good doctor was able to survive in his profession. He seemed to suffer nearly as much as his patients.

"But there's got to be something..." Decimus, still holding Patricia's hand, struggled to get the words out.

Patricia slowly lifted a feeble finger to her husband's

lips. "Sssshhh dear." Her words were barely audible as her hand fell back down to the bed. "There is nothing you or anybody can do now." A moment's silence filled the room as young Decimus struggled to hold back a sob.

Patricia gathered the last of her strength and continued. "This is where I want to spend my final moments." She was struck by a fit of coughing that seemed to drain the last of her dwindling energy. Both Decimus and the doctor watched her, helplessly. It sounded painful… looked painful. And there was absolutely nothing they could do.

The coughing stopped followed by equally painful silence. Then Patricia struggled to continue speaking. "I want to be here with my family, in my home, where I spent the happiest days of my life." Another feeble cough and then, "I need to be here."

She smiled weakly, despite the pain that wracked her body and the sadness in her heart. As old Croome watched the scene unfold, he noticed that a buoyant young nurse had taken the place of Patricia's doctor. Croome could not remember the nurse's name or anything else about her, but he did remember what happened next. It was the worst moment of his life, and he now had to witness it again. He had never forgotten what it felt like to lose his wife, his lover, his best friend. He would never have wished for anybody to experience that horrible pain once, let alone a second time.

Silence enshrouded the room, an eternal silence. Patricia was gone. Decimus's soul seemed to leave with her. He slumped over in his chair and gripped her hand even harder as if he could pull her back into the room, as if he could keep her from escaping, could physically stop her from ever leaving him. But she was gone. The nurse gently placed a compassionate hand on Decimus's shoulder.

Old Croome wanted to look away. He had no desire to experience this moment again. But he couldn't help watching as the kindly nurse put her hand on young Decimus's back, trying in vain to comfort him. It was a moment that old Croome didn't remember. In fact, he didn't have many good memories after this point in his life. It was as if he lost the ability to see goodness in the world.

But he did remember what happened next. Young Decimus stood up, his hands balled into fists and his body shaking with intense sorrow. He slowly looked around the room at Patricia's beloved Halloween decorations littering every wall, window, end table and bookshelf. And then, like a deranged maniac, he flew into a rage. He went from calm and grief stricken to complete lunacy as he began tearing bats from the ceiling, ripping witches off the wall and flailing at plastic spiders crawling through fake cobwebs.

The nurse had no idea what to do. She also began shaking hysterically and trying desperately to console Decimus. "It's okay. She's gone now." Even after years of dealing with similar situations, she struggled to find the appropriate words. "She's in a better place." There were no 'right' words.

Decimus was inconsolable. He continued on his rampage, consumed with grief and lashing out at everything that reminded him of his life with Patricia. He desperately wanted to stop the intense pain that crushed him from the inside out. He was driven by some inner voice that seemed to be telling him to let it all out or he would explode with grief.

The nurse backed away from the sorrow-stricken young husband. She had witnessed intense bereavement before but never anything quite this profound. "Decimus!! Remember, your daughter is sleeping in the next room."

She stammered, still watching him closely, afraid of what he might do next.

And with that, Decimus simply crumpled back into a nearby chair looking helpless, hopeless and depleted. "My daughter. Oh God, my daughter." His voice faded from a whisper to oblivion. "I am so sorry Eve. So, so very sorry." All life seemed to drain from his languid body.

For a change, even the Spirit of Halloween Past was subdued, almost sympathetic. His previously demonic eyes gazed upon Croome with an uncharacteristic compassion. "Has this one dark Halloween eclipsed all of the joyous ones?"

Croome did not reply. He just stared at his younger self, remembering his own horrible pain but not the havoc he had wreaked upon others on that fateful night. He had tried to block out all such memories both good and bad. Seeing it again was nearly as painful as living through it the first time.

When the Spirit hesitantly held out its sinewy fingers, Croome slowly and painfully reached up with a half-hearted grasp. "Please take me back to my home. I cannot bear another memory as painful as the ones I have just seen."

"I'm afraid we have one last Halloween to visit." Even the spirit seemed reluctant to continue the evening's forays. Croome had neither the energy nor will to protest. He closed his eyes in an attempt to block out the overwhelming sorrow.

As with the previous excursions, Croome could feel the wind rushing by and the sensation of floating on air. However, with his eyes closed he was unable to see the landscape beneath them. His other senses seemed to take up the slack and Croome heard the distant sounds of children's voices below. His sense of smell seemed especially keen, and he detected the familiar odors of autumn. Each scent reminded him of death: dead leaves, skeletal trees and emaciated crops.

As they set down, Croome was hesitant to open his eyes, fearful of what sights would confront him next. But when he finally dared to glance about, a familiar room greeted him with much less Halloween frivolity than the past ones. Even though it was the same house and the same living room, it lacked the previous holiday adornments and cheer.

A much older, sterner looking Decimus Croome was

engaged in heated debate with a beautiful young lady. She was trying with all her might to persuade the scowling Croome. "But Daddy." It was always 'Daddy' when she wanted something. "Why can't I go trick-or-treating with my friends? Halloween only comes around once a year. It's not fair to keep me here all by myself."

"You are too old to be trick-or-treating. Besides, someone has to stay here to pass out treats to the costumed beasts. You know I have to go back to the store tonight."

Young Eve Croome stomped her feet in a teen rage. "Too old? I'm only thirteen." She pointed to her birthday cake on the table, a cake she had made for herself. "If I can't have a birthday party, at least you could let me go out trick-or-treating with my friends."

"Let's not argue Eve." Decimus pleaded with his daughter. "You can invite one of your friends over to pass out treats with you. You like passing out treats to the neighbor kids."

"Treats? You call carrots and celery sticks treats? It's embarrassing to pass out such lame *treats* at Halloween. Who wants vegetables on the one day everyone else is giving away candy? And besides, why would my friends want to spend Halloween here?" She pointed around the room. "You won't even let me put up Halloween decorations. Who would want to spend the night here instead of going out with friends and getting candy and seeing all the *FUN LOOKING* houses that are *DECORATED* for Halloween?"

Decimus reached out toward the top of his daughter's head and then quickly jerked his hand back as if he had received an electrical shock. He couldn't remember the last time he had shown physical affection to his daughter… or anyone for that matter. He couldn't bring himself to show emotion, and he wasn't about to get into a debate with Eve.

It wasn't as if he was completely ignorant of his daughter's feelings. Deep inside, he remembered how much her mother had loved Halloween. But he also knew how much Halloween could hurt. Each year it brought back a harvest of candy apple memories. But each year those memories turned out to be rotten to the core, sugar coated in sweet syrup but filled with nasty, writhing worms of disappointment and dejection.

Decimus slipped his lanky arms into the sleeves of his well-worn plaid jacket and prepared to head out the door on his way back to the store. "If you run out of carrots, there are more in the refrigerator. Don't forget to wash and peel them. And only give out one per child."

"Who's going to want more than one? Besides hardly anyone comes here anyway."

"And don't give anything to teenagers or kids without costumes. They shouldn't even be out freeloading."

Eve stood at the door and watched her father walk away practically knocking over an enthusiastic group of young trick-or-treaters on his way down the porch steps. She hollered out to her rapidly disappearing dad. "Everybody throws your carrots away when they get home anyway."

The same band of costumed kids that Croome nearly bowled over like ninepins heard the dreaded c-word. "Carrots?? For Halloween?!" They chanted in unison and quickly retreated to join their guardian parents who stood sentinel on the sidewalk.

Eve, still standing in the doorway, glanced at the hovering parents then fired one last salvo at the retreating plaid-jacketed back of her father. "Even the parents throw away your carrot sticks."

The Spirit of Halloween Past stared silently at Old

Croome whose shoulders seemed to slump under a heavy burden. "Carrots? On Halloween?"

Decimus Croome ignored his inquisitive companion and stared silently at his daughter as she slammed the door. He no longer needed the Spirit or anyone else to point out his shortcomings. "All those birthdays and Halloweens. Where did they go? Why did I let them slip away?"

The Spirit knew that Croome's questions weren't directed at anybody but Croome himself. After a moment of silence, he turned to his glum looking companion. "We should be going. I'm afraid our time is over, and I must get you back to your cat… and your next visitor."

Old Croome was nearly comatose and allowed the Spirit to lead him away like a dog on a leash. He didn't even seem to notice when one of the spiders crawled off the Spirit's robe and crawled across his sunken face. He probably wouldn't have noticed if the entire menagerie of spiders would have spun a cocoon around his body and wrapped him up like a living, breathing mummy.

He barely remembered anything after that. Before he knew what was happening, he was curled up on his bed trying desperately to deal with the swirl of foul memories suddenly flung to the forefront of his consciousness. All the good memories from the first half of his life were completely eclipsed by his dreadful deeds and actions from the second half.

# Chapter 9 - Witch in the Kitchen

Croome tried to find solace in sleep, but the voices in his head were every bit as real and haunting as the pumpkin-headed spirit.

*"There was nothing more they could do for me in the hospital."*

*"This is where I want to spend my last moments."*

*"She's gone now."*

*"Why can't I go trick-or-treating with my friends?"*

*"Who would want to spend Halloween here?"*

The maddening murmurs became a deafening roar until he could take it no more and buried his head under a pillow in a futile attempt to shut out the turbulent static.

But it was to no avail.

Croome tried to focus on the good times, the wonderful Halloweens before sweet Patricia departed this world and his life. But he couldn't seem to rid his mind of the maddening voices that haunted him relentlessly. A dominant chorus of hostile speculation filled his head and clouded his memory.

Nor could he stop thinking of the spirits yet to come. Would they reveal happy times or sad times? What more could they show him? What if they showed him even worse visions of his life? He was unsure if he could handle any more repulsive revelations of his own atrocities.

Finally the angst-ridden Croome could take it no longer. As long as he lay idly in bed, his mind would allow him no peace. He had to get up and do something, even if it meant just rambling about his vacuous old house. He was compelled to do anything that might help remove the heavy burden from his heart.

He swung his lanky legs off the bed, and his feet sought warmth in a ragged but comfortable pair of unkempt slippers. He pulled a tatty old checkered bathrobe over his shoulders and padded down the stairs toward the kitchen. He briefly hoped that the next spirit would not be able to find him if he wasn't asleep in his bed. But then he realized the silliness of that idea and pish-poshed his own nonsensical thinking.

As Croome approached the kitchen, it appeared there was a light wastefully glowing near the sink. This minor extravagance was a major annoyance for an old cheapskate like Croome who carefully guarded each kilowatt of electricity that squeaked through his precious power grid. A penny saved was a penny earned, and a penny squandered was unforgivable.

However as the old skinflint drew nearer to the kitchen, he realized there was something strange about the light emanating from within. It was neither white nor yellow but seemed to emit a stygian purple hue. It reminded him of those ridiculous hippie black lights from his childhood.

He soon stopped worrying about having left a cursed light on in the kitchen; for the hellish hue that emanated from within was definitely more troublesome than a few wasted watts of electricity. Croome crept to the kitchen entrance and cautiously peered around the corner. It had been a strange evening so far and was about to get exponentially stranger. For someone or some-*thing* was in the kitchen… *without Dinah, and they most certainly weren't strummin' on an old banjo.*

Standing with its back toward him bending over the stove was a lone figure dressed mostly in black. Everything about this figure was disturbing. The clothing was bizarre, the tall peaked hat was unusual and, strangest of all, its disturbing radiance saturated the room with an eerie glow while simultaneously draining it of all light. Croome had never seen anything that looked even vaguely similar to the character that was currently plaguing his kitchen.

After his previous experiences of the evening, he knew this must be the second spirit that Patricia had warned him about. But this one looked as different from the last spirit as night from day.

'Witch' was the first word that came to Croome's mind. The creature resembled a classical witch in so many regards.

He assumed it was a woman, for she was wearing a long black dress or possibly a gown. Her hat was tall, narrow and peaked with numerous creases and a slight bend in the middle. The hair that flowed out from under the hat was black but more of a glistening black than either the robe or the hat. As he looked closer, he noticed some streaks of purple and silver in the hair and... Spiders? More spiders? What's up with these ghosts and their abominable spiders?

And to top off the witchly costume was a black cat, looking up at the woman while glissading under her gown and slinking around the orange striped leotards that clung steadfastly to her legs.

"Nice cat, but horrible kitchen supplies." Came a high-pitched, raspy voice from the witch. She didn't bother to turn around but kept stirring what looked like a bubbling cauldron of steaming brew on the stovetop.

"And let's get a few things straight. I'm not a witch. I'm the Ghost of Halloween Present who just happens to dress like your stereotypical notions of a witch." She reached down and scooped up Croome's black cat in her left hand and continued stirring the cauldron with her right.

"And it's not a cauldron. Once again, you're projecting your own narrow-minded stereotypes onto others. That's very judgmental you know?"

Croome stood frozen in place, intrigued by the stranger in his kitchen but wholly afraid of making one false move or uttering one objectionable phrase.

"And finally," she turned to face him, and he was startled by her beautiful face. He had expected...

"I know. You expected to see an ugly old crone." And with that, her face briefly reverted from strikingly beautiful to startlingly hideous complete with leathery skin, long pointy nose and a hairy wart sticking out of the end. And in her gnarled right hand, she held what appeared to be…

"No it's not a magic wand." And like that, her beautiful face had returned complete with a mischievous grin. She pointed the thin rod at Croome, and what appeared to be a miniature bolt of lightning shot out of the end and zapped him in the haunches causing him to yelp and jump a half-foot in the air.

"It's a magic cattle prod. Much more useful and high tech than the old wands." Then the Witc… Spirit stroked the arching spine of Black Magic. "Speaking of stereotypes, I **am** kind of fond of black cats." Her grin grew even broader as she set the contented cat down on Croome's old, yellowing linoleum floor.

Croome was confused by the whole *Ghosts of Halloween* concept. "I thought I was supposed to be visited by three *ghosts* tonight? You.. you don't really look.."

"Like a ghost?" The witch finished his sentence for him and started cackling in classical witch style. Then her appearance changed again into that of a shrewd-looking salesman complete with slicked back hair, square jaw, shining white teeth and a bamboo cane in his hand. "That's the ticket. I'm a ghost, I'm a witch. I'm two Halloween freaks in one. But order today, and you'll get not two but three Halloween demons."

With that, she changed into a howling werewolf with thick brown hair all over her face and body, sharp claws and ravenous fangs. "Act now and we'll throw in a Transylvanian vampire for free." She became a campy, white-skinned vampire with two impressive fangs and a jet-black widow's peak.

Then, just as quickly, she changed back to the beautiful witch. "Ghosts, witches? Who's keeping track? It's not the messenger, but the message that counts. So call me whatever you want; the Ghost of Halloween Present, the Witch of Halloween Present. Just don't call me late for dinner. With that, the witch reached down into the cauldron and pulled out a fat, wriggling rat by its oversized tail. She held it over her wide-opened mouth as if she was about to pop an appetizer in her mouth. But then she glanced down at Magic the cat and let out another mischievous cackle.

Without warning she flicked the rotund rodent down onto the floor in front of the startled cat. Out of sheer instinct, Black Magic arched her back and let out a half-hearted hiss. Not missing a beat, the repugnant rat belched out an even more impressive hiss that bordered on a roar.

Black Magic wore a look of surprise on her face, but it was soon replaced by a scared look that was soon followed by sheer terror. With a pair of oversized eyeballs and a whimpering meow, she began to back away from her intimidating adversary. The sharp-toothed rat towered over Magic and seemed about ready to pounce when the witch sent a miniature bolt of lightning from her magic cattle prod right into the rodent's ample belly.

The rat glowed for a brief instant then immediately shrank to normal size. Once again, the startled black cat was wide-eyed with amazement. Now, rather than retreating, she began advancing as her look of dismay quickly switched to one of glee. Her feline lips curled into a malicious grin, and the chase was on as the newly emboldened Black Magic obviously relished the return of her traditional role as daring assailant rather than scaredy cat prey.

The game of cat-and-mouse went on for a few harried moments until the Witchly Spirit grew tired of her own fun and games. "Now let's get going. Time's a-wastin'" She commanded as she suddenly seemed much closer to Croome, and he couldn't tell if she'd floated or walked or just magically zapped herself into her new proximity. His head was swimming, and the witch seemed to like it that way.

"Ya got a spare broom?" She asked.

"Do I have a…?" At first Croome couldn't wrap his addled brain around what she was asking. Then, as if in a fog, he realized it was a simple question. "I-i-In the closet." Croome said, pointing toward a door off to one side of the kitchen.

"Of course you've got a broom." She said and, with a snap of her fingers, the closet door swung open and a tattered old broom flew out of the closet and swooped directly into her extended hand.

She inspected the broom with a critical eye and barked out, "You call this a broom. You get 'em at cost and this is the best you can do?"

With that, she rose into the air, snapped the fingers of her free hand, and the broom flew behind and then underneath her. She immediately started flying wildly around the room. She zig-zagged, loop-de-looped and roller coastered from one end of the kitchen to the other and everywhere in between. She looked like a rookie cowpoke riding his first bucking bronco. And then she careened haphazardly in the direction of the awkwardly backpedaling Decimus Croome. He put up his hands as if he had the slightest chance of stopping the out-of-control enchantress.

But she just kept coming directly at him like a runaway locomotive. For a moment Croome felt just like the stereotypical damsel-in-distress, tied to the railroad tracks and completely helpless. Then, at the last minute, he made a diving leap for the softest spot on the otherwise hard kitchen floor. He crash-landed right on the small kitchen rug that slid madly across the linoleum floor causing Croome to smack his head into the nearby kitchen cabinets.

Croome sprawled haphazardly atop the crumpled kitchen rug and when he looked up, he saw the spirit standing over him examining the broomstick, muttering to herself. "Whoever came up with the idea that these could be used for transportation?" With that she broke the brittle broom over her right knee. "And imagine the splinters! Talk about a pain in the posterior!"

Croome had no idea whether to take her seriously or not. His only spiritous experience had been with the Ghost of Halloween Past, but ol' pumpkin head was night-and-day different from this chatty witch. So he decided to gradually change the subject as he slowly and carefully made his way back onto his feet. "So how do we get from here to... wherever? Should I hold your hand or ..."

"How dare you get fresh with little ol' innocent me." The witch swooned and struck a deep southern drawl. Just as quickly as she'd changed from the beautiful witch to the old crone and back again, she took on the appearance of a southern belle complete with a hoop skirt, white gloves and a straw bonnet.

Before Croome could react to the latest shape-shifting episode, the witch switched back to her usual self, pointed at something directly beneath Croome's feet and said, "I think that will work just fine."

And with no warning, Croome felt the kitchen rug moving underneath him and then, BAM!! He fell flat on his fanny. Croome expected the pratfall to be painful, but it was like falling onto a giant pillow. He looked around, startled. The first thing he noticed was that he was now lying across the rug on which he had recently been standing upright. But it took on a whole new shape. The weight of his own body seemed to have indented the surface, and the rest of it was curling up around him. But the most astonishing part was yet to come. As Croome looked around, he realized the rug he had been standing on was now flying in mid-air.

To his horror, he realized that it was not just flying but flying out of control. With the startled Croome hanging on for dear life, the flying flooring made a mad dash for the ceiling. Just before crashing through the roof, it wildly detoured on a collision course for the nearest wall. At the last moment the careening carpet changed course and flew directly onto a cluttered countertop sending dirty dishes and silverware clattering in every direction and crashing onto the floor. Finally, the out-of-control rug came to a stop in the kitchen sink with Croome's posterior planted directly in the middle; and, to make matters worse, the faucet suddenly began spraying water all over his lap.

Croome hastily reached up to turn off the faucet. In the process, he accidentally turned on the spray nozzle, which then squirted outward into the kitchen. With great dismay,

Croome noticed that it had sprayed a jet stream of water onto the astonished witch. Her body immediately started hissing and steaming and shrinking into the floor. She let out a blood-curdling scream and wailed, "No!! Help meeee!! I'm meltttttttingggg." She shot Croome an evil glare and croaked, "Now look what you've done you wretched fool. Noooooooo!!! Curse you and your little cat, too."

While Black Magic arched her back into an imposing mound, Croome frantically fumbled to turn off the spray. "Oh my goodness, I'm sorry. I.. I ... I didn't mean to…"

Before Croome's astonished eyes the witch seemed to melt into the floor leaving only a small puddle and a tall, crumpled witch's hat where she had once stood. Croome was horrified and completely speechless.

He slumped back into the sink and stared straight ahead. What had he done? What could he do now? He had destroyed one of the spirits who had come to help him. Silence descended upon Croome. He felt helpless and hopeless. After all that he had seen and learned from the Ghost of Halloween Past, he couldn't help but wonder what he would have learned from the witch.

His lamentations soon turned to astonishment however

as he noticed the crumpled rug seemingly coming to life. Croome quickly and awkwardly hauled his undignified carcass out of the sink and watched, dumfounded, as the rug appeared to slowly rise off the floor; but unlike before, it didn't look as if it was flying. Instead, it looked like it was being lifted from underneath.

Suddenly it flew straight up into the air and directly toward Croome. Out of the silence came a derisive cackling and the rug dropped to the floor revealing a hysterically howling witch.

"Now that was entertaining." The witch chortled. "You should have seen the look on your face. You looked like you'd just seen a ghost." Poof... she disappeared again, but only for a second then, "... a dead ghost." She reappeared behind him and wailed in his ear nearly bringing him to his knees with shock and fright.

Before Croome had time to react, the witch disappeared and reappeared, floating upside down over his head. She continued babbling semi-coherently as if these upside-down conversations were daily routines. " You know, I've never understood how a few drops of water could melt a witch." She was no longer hovering above him but actually sitting lightly atop his head as if he was a human reclining chair. "But hey, since I'm more of a ghost than a witch, wha'do I know?"

Croome ducked his head and pushed the witch away as though she was a pesky fly. "Don't you have something to show me?" He snorted, as the witch lazily floated across the room like a Halloween helium balloon.

"My aren't we grumpy. Someone woke up on the wrong side of reality." The witch slowly glided to a stop on top of Croome's flying rug. "But I suppose you're right. We've got places to go and people to stalk." With that, she snapped her fingers and Croome suddenly found himself awkwardly sitting behind the witch, on the rug, as it rapidly flew out of the kitchen, up the stairs and through the wide-open bedroom window. All the while, Croome clung to the tassels of his precarious perch as if his life was hanging by a thread. And perhaps it was.

The unlikely pair flew over neighborhoods that had replaced the forests from Croome's childhood past. Most of the houses were gaily embellished with Halloween ornaments of all shapes and sizes. Some of them were illuminated, some were inflated; they covered the spectrum of scariness from harmless kiddy cartoon characters to creepy half-dead ghouls with blood-soaked fangs and claws. None of them looked familiar or appealing to Croome.

Trick-or-treaters gradually dribbled forth from the houses on their somewhat frenzied pursuit of Halloween sweet treats. Each was festooned according to their age from cute and cozy costumes on toddlers, to ghoulish and garish garments on the older teens.

From the residential neighborhoods Croome and his Wiccan guide veered toward the quaint little Main Street where most of the local businesses were also decorated for the holiday. Their windows were painted with Halloween characters and hung with orange, purple and black lights. The local bookstore was adorned with Halloween tomes and the clothing stores displayed Halloween-themed mannequins. Each storefront wore some sort of Halloween adornment, from mild to wild, with the exception of one drab structure.

The witchly Spirit turned to Croome with a comical look of mock disgust. "Hummmm. I spy with my little eye, one boringly bland business."

Old Decimus had never noticed what an eyesore

Croome's Hardware had become. He had never seen it from this birds-eye view and realized that it was indeed rather dull looking in comparison to the neighboring merchants. His normal reply would have been to point out that he was in the hardware business rather than the entertainment business. But considering what he knew about his spectral companion, he was pretty sure that answer would be deemed unacceptable.

The Spirit of Halloween Present stood up on the flying carpet and faced Croome, her arms pointing to the left and right. "Your pilot has indicated that we are prepared to make our final descent into Croome's humdrum hardware store. Please be sure that your seat belts are fastened and all carry-on luggage is safely secured in the overhead bins. On behalf of Wiccan Airlines we'd like to thank you for flying with us. We know you have a choice in flying rugs, and we appreciate that you chose us. Please turn off all electrical devices and hang on for dear life. In case of a water landing, your inflated ego acts as a flotation device."

And with that, the carpet took a precipitous dive leaving the spiritual stewardess suspended in mid-air and Croome screaming like a geriatric toddler as he plummeted toward the oncoming storefront. Just as they were about to crash through a boringly spartan plate glass window, the blazing carpet veered into the doorway that had just been opened by a departing customer who, of course, was completely unaware of the plummeting scareliner.

Croome's gut-wrenching descent screeched to a sudden halt directly in front of an unassuming and unsuspecting family who stood near a hopelessly outdated cash register near the front of the hardware store. Croome's capricious conveyance gently touched down as lightly as an ostrich feather. In both coloration and demeanor, Croome resembled a seasick salamander as he shakily stepped down onto the grayish-brown hardwood floor.

The witch reappeared with a poof and stood beside Croome. "Recognize anyone?" She asked, as innocently as if they had just arrived via taxi.

Croome managed a tremulous smile at the sight of these familiar folks standing in front of him. "It is my faithful employee Sam Bobbich and…" Croome's grin grew even wider. "That's his beautiful wife and magnificent son, young Tommy."

Croome's newfound admiration of the Bobbich family

did not seem to be mutual as Mrs. Bobbich stood with one hand on her hip and the other waving a finger in front of her husband's wide-eyed face. "Sam Bobbich." She lectured, in an unusually stern voice. "For the past two months, your son has been talking about nothing but trick-or-treating with his father on Halloween. And now… now, you tell us that your…" She glanced down at Tommy and chose her next words carefully. "… your slave-driving boss is making you work on this special holiday night?"

Croome couldn't help but wonder what was so special about this particular Halloween and was even more perplexed by young Tommy Bobbich's shining bald pate as he watched faithful Sam rub his smiling son's shaven head.

"Now dear. Technically Halloween isn't an official holiday, and Mr. Croome needed me to work the store this evening, as he does every evening." Sam looked guiltily at his wife.

"Needed you? He didn't need you to work tonight. What better does that miserly old coot have to do on this evening but to pass out a few carrot sticks to unsuspecting trick-or-treaters who don't know any better than to avoid his cursed house on Halloween?"

Upon hearing 'carrot sticks' young Tommy Bobbich wrinkled his nose. "Does Mr. Croome really hand out carrot sticks on Halloween?" He asked his father.

"Why yes he does, Tommy. Mr. Croome distributes the healthiest treats in town." Sam Bobbich averted his gaze from the uncharitable glare of his wife. Then he quickly changed the subject. "I'm sorry I won't be able to join you on your trick-or-treating rounds, Tommy. But hopefully I'll be able to meet you at the Halloween party later tonight."

Tommy's eyes brightened at the mention of the upcoming Halloween festivities. "I can't wait for the party. It will be almost as much fun as trick-or-treating. Do you promise you'll be there Dad?"

"I certainly hope so, Tommy. It was so nice of the Tates to invite us to their Halloween party, now wasn't it?"

Croome, who was listening to the Bobbich conversation with great curiosity, perked up at the mention of his daughter's name. He had forgotten all about the party. (The party he hadn't planned to attend.) He glanced sheepishly at his cryptic companion as he gradually became aware of the evening's theme. He began to realize that he had been ignorant of his own dismal Halloween temperament.

"You said you had a costume idea for me, Daddy?" Young Tommy Bobbich looked expectantly toward his father.

"So I did. So I did." Sam Bobbich couldn't help but smile at the eager look in his son's eyes. "I just happen to have the perfect costume for you in the back room. You just wait here while I…"

"Why don't you run into the backroom and see if you can find the costume, Tommy?" Belinda Bobbich interrupted her husband.

"But Mr. Croome says I'm not supposed to run in his store." Tommy glanced from parent to parent, unsure of how to proceed.

"Well Mr. Croome can…" Belinda's voice rose at least a dozen decibels.

"Mr. Croome is absolutely right Tommy." It was Sam's turn to interrupt his wife. "The costume is in a white plastic bag on the countertop in the back room. Don't peak inside until you're back out here."

Sam knew that his wife had information to share about Tommy's visit to the doctor's office so he added, "And could you please sweep the sawdust off the floor while you're back there? I'm sure Mr. Croome would appreciate it, and so would I." No matter how rudely Decimus Croome treated Tommy, the young lad seemed to enjoy helping around the store in hopes that maybe some day the old man would take notice and miraculously say something appreciative.

"I'll make sure to put the broom away this time so Mr. Croome doesn't get mad again." Tommy remarked as he disappeared into the back room.

"I'd like to put Mr. Croome's broom…"

Sam interrupted his wife again. "How did Tommy's doctor appointment go today?"

The change in Belinda Bobbich was instantaneous. Her head went down and her shoulders slumped. It was as if someone had yanked the spine out of her back. She only had two words to say, at first. "Why Tommy?" Then almost inaudibly, she repeated those two words. "Why Tommy?"

She didn't want an answer, and Sam knew better than to try and give her one. Instead, he wrapped his arms around her and held her close. He knew exactly how she felt, but he knew better than to say so. She didn't want him to compare their feelings or to even acknowledge her feelings. She just needed his shoulder and his arms and his love.

All day, she had to be strong for Tommy. All day she had to put on a happy face and listen to doctors and pretend to be strong. All day, she had to hold her emotions in check until they filled her to overflowing. But she could hold them no longer and, in the arms of her husband, she let them out. Not in an explosion of rage but in a whisper of sorrow. "I hate leukemia!!" She sobbed. And once again, she repeated herself in a tremulous murmur. "I hate leukemia with all of my heart!!"

For a moment they just embraced, hating leukemia and loving each other; but above all, loving their son beyond the scope of any words. The last thing Belinda wanted to talk about was white blood cell counts, red blood cell counts and chemotherapy. She wanted a break from anything to do with cancer and doctors and hospitals.

But even more, she wanted her son to be better again. She wanted him to be able to play like other kids and to be a happy little boy again and to live without the specter of pain constantly haunting his every waking moment. She wanted him to be able to eat a meal without losing half of it to a disgusting disease that he called pukemia.

So many thoughts, emotions and conflicts filled her mind, but all she could say was, "I hate pukemia with all my heart."

As Belinda struggled to regain her composure and put on her suit of armor, Sam took a step back but still held her trembling shoulders in his strong hands. "And you love Tommy with all your heart."

Belinda Bobbich looked directly into her husband's eyes and said, in a voice heavy with worry and heartache, "Yes I do. And so do you. But will that be enough? How will we keep paying the medical bills? We've already taken out a second mortgage on the house and we're behind on those payments."

Everything she said was true, and Sam knew it. But he refused to think about it. He refused to think about anything but his son, his daughter and his wife. "We'll be fine." He said. "Tommy will get better, and everything will work out for the best."

Belinda wanted so badly to believe it was true. But she knew that it wasn't that simple. And she knew Sam was only putting on a brave face for the sake of his family.

Just then Tommy emerged from the back room, smiling as always. Smiling through the pain. Smiling through the heartache.

*If only I had his courage*, Sam and Belinda each thought with one mind.

Tommy was so excited to open the costume bag that he didn't notice a final tear falling from his mom's cheek. Sam Bobbich gave his wife's hand one last reassuring squeeze and turned his attention to his son. He couldn't cure Tommy's leukemia or remove the heavy burden of sorrow and responsibility from his wife, but he could do everything in his power to make the fleeting good times last as long as possible.

Sam slowly began pulling items from the white plastic bag, one at a time, and dramatically holding them above his head for all to see. Tommy's face lit up as each costume part was gradually revealed. It became a guessing game with Tommy trying to figure out what character would wear such a costume.

The first item to appear above Sam's head was a black felt-tip pen. Tommy scrunched his face and scratched his chin as if deep in thought. "A writer? A teacher?" He guessed.

"Not even close," his dad laughed. Then he pulled a white sailor's cap out of the bag.

Tommy had no idea what to think. He tried to make a connection between the pen and the cap but was completely stymied. "This is too hard. Can we just dump the bag out and see it all at once?"

Sam shook his head and pulled a corncob pipe out of the bag. Tommy was still puzzled so his mom made a guess. "Mark Twain? It's got to be Mark Twain. He was a writer, so the pen fits his character. I think he smoked a corncob pipe or at least some of his characters did. And I'm pretty sure he wore a white hat when he was a riverboat captain."

"That is a very good guess and I must admit, you are absolutely…" Sam was enjoying himself every bit as much as his son and wife. "Wrong." He winked at his wife who had been totally convinced she had figured it out.

Next, Sam pulled out what looked like an empty spinach can and a black shirt with a wide, red collar. "I had to have the shirt specially made, but your aunt Jenny helped me with that part."

Both Tommy and his mother had to think for a moment, and then Mrs. Bobbich let out a whoop. "I know who it is."

Tommy still had a puzzled look on his face so his mom started firing clues in his direction. "He's a sailor. He smokes a pipe. He eats spinach and has big muscles. He's one of the old cartoon characters your dad likes to watch on…"

"Popeye!!" Tommy yelped, pumping a victory fist in the air. "It's perfect." He ran over and grabbed the sailor's cap from the costume pile. "I've already got a Popeye haircut." He jammed the hat on his head and began singing, "I'm Popeye the sailor man."

Tommy's father reached out and wrapped one of his hands around Tommy's upper arm. "It looks like you already have Popeye's muscles!!" Followed by a very poor imitation of Popeye's laugh.

"Good thing you've been eating your spinach." Added Tommy's mom who welcomed every opportunity to convince her son to eat his veggies.

———————————

Of course none of the Bobbich family members had any idea that they were being observed from above. Old Croome was watching the entire scene with an uncharacteristic grin on his face.

"It's curious how such a pish-posh holiday as Halloween seems to brighten the lives of so many people." The pointy-hatted Spirit turned towards Croome. "Including a certain dottering old sourpuss."

Croome continued beaming. "I had no idea that it took so little to make a child like Tommy happy."

"Aaahh! It would appear that you might have underestimated the magic of Halloween."

Croome only nodded his head and continued staring at the youngest member of the Bobbich family. That smile was so genuine, so powerful, so contagious. "Such courage." He muttered, mostly to himself. "I had no idea he was sick. And yet look at how happy he seems."

The witchly spirit recognized a teachable moment when she heard it, and in her wisest and most thoughtful voice replied, "Wellll ddduuuuuhhhhh!!?!!" Her eyes spun crazily in their sockets while her tongue hung limply out the side of her mouth.

Croome ignored her antics and continued his ruminations. "Maybe I misjudged the power of this holiday that I tried so hard to ignore. But it's been such a burden. When my dear sweet Patricia died, it's almost as if Halloween died right along with her."

Croome grew silent as he continued looking down upon the Bobbich family, together in both pain and joy. He had built a wall and shut out the world around himself. And now, like the ghosts that were visiting him, Halloween was gradually coming back to life and haunting him in a most unusual but not altogether unpleasant way.

"It is time for us to move on." the spirit nudged Croome with her magic cattle prod. He barely noticed as he reluctantly stepped onto the hovering carpet while continuing to stare at the Bobbich family. He realized that the joy of Halloween had not departed this world. It had only departed his world.

# Chapter 10 - Halloween Presence

As soon as the Spirit joined Croome, they were abruptly whisked into the air, once again knocking Croome on his backside before floating out the door and back into the heart of town.

"Where to now, Spirit?" Croome asked, trying unsuccessfully to hide the apprehension in his voice.

Before answering, the mischievous Spirit decided to have some more fun with her inquisitive passenger. In the snap of her long, slender fingers a cowboy hat flew onto her head and suddenly she was adorned like a Wild West buckaroo. She reached down and grabbed hold of the flying carpet as it took on the shape of a bucking bronco. Croome nearly flew off the back as they shot up and down then bolted left and right with the cowpoke Witch yeehawing at the top of her lungs.

About the time Croome thought he was going to either toss his cookies or be tossed off the back of the bucking carpet, the witch snapped her fingers again and the steed turned back into your standard, run-of-the-mill flying rug. The Spirit still had on her cowboy attire, though, as she turned to Croome and drawled, "Well podner, we're moseyin' on over to another neighborhood to visit some young fellows you may recognize from a recent encounter." By this time Croome had forgotten his question and was looking a bit green around the gills.

With one last snap of her fingers, the Spirit was back to her normal garb and the flying duo departed Main Street headed toward a warren of quaint old houses in the residential section of town. Croome peered over the edge of the volatile vehicle only vaguely aware of their location.

"I have never been here before." Croome mumbled, a bit embarrassed of being lost in his own small town.

"Maybe you've never been to this particular house," the witch suggested, "but…" Without warning the cruising rug rapidly rolled itself up like a window shade with Croome and his companion squished inside, as snug as two bugs in a burrito.

"Now isn't this cozy?" A somewhat stifled witch pondered aloud, her nose squashed flat against Croome's face. And then, the tightly packed pair dove straight toward the unfamiliar house and, before crashing into the roof, popped down the chimney, unrolling like a spinning top as soon as it hit the floor and unceremoniously releasing its dizzy occupants into a spacious but drab living room.

The witch picked up her previous thread of conversation as if nothing had happened. "I did not say you had been to this house before, but do those young creatures look familiar?" The witch pointed toward two young gentlemen that Croome recognized immediately. He remembered both their costumes and the boys themselves. And as soon as they began talking, he recalled their voices also.

"Aaahh, the two young lads from the Home Emporium." From the sheepish tone of Croome's voice, it was obvious that he not only remembered the boys but also remembered how he had treated them. He looked away from the spirit in an attempt to hide his reddening face. "It looks like our young friend got off the hook okay."

Indeed, standing near the inside front door of the house were the two youngsters Croome had accosted in the hardware store. They seemed to be involved in a heavy conversation with a couple adults Croome assumed were their parents.

"But I don't want to go trick-or-treating." Said the

smaller of the two boys. "What if the monster is out there?" He instinctively stepped toward the sheltering shadow of his father as if the "monster" might be somewhere in the room.

The older, slightly larger boy crossed his arms in disgust. "How many times do I have to tell you? That guy wasn't a monster. He was a jerk."

Croome had no doubt about what 'monster' the boys were talking and, although he knew it was impossible, he felt as if the older boy was glaring right at him. Of course that was just his imagination. But the hostile stare from his spiritual guide was plenty real and plenty vicious.

The father placed his hand upon the younger boy's shoulder. "Your brother is right." He knelt down so that he was at eye-level with his son. "It's Halloween, and there are lots of pretend monsters out there. But you don't have to worry about real monsters."

The boys' mother joined the conversation. " Everything will be just fine. There are no monsters around here." Her tone of voice dropped slightly as she added, "Just an ignorant bully who is going to get a piece of my mind the next time I go into Croome's Hardware store."

Almost as if mirroring the actions of the little boy, an invisible Croome took a furtive step back behind his guardian Spirit like a young cub hiding behind his mama bear.

The father sounded slightly calmer but every bit as agitated as his wife. "Well I don't know about giving Mr. Croome a piece of my mind, but I can assure you I WON'T be giving him my business any more."

The spirit was staring at Croome, tapping her feet as if waiting for an explanation.

"I was just having a little fun."

The stare became a glare.

"Possibly I was having a little too much fun."

The glare intensified.

"Okay. I may have gotten carried away."

The spirit crossed her arms in disgust and continued glaring.

"I did get carried away. Okay? I'm a horrible rotten person and a big bully who has learned his lesson."

Suddenly the carpet jerked forward and Croome once again found himself flat on his back, and the spirit's glare turned into a smirk.

"Now look who's being a bully." Croome mumbled under his breath to both the spirit and the flying carpet.

Hoping to distract the spirit and get some relief from her evil glare, Croome quickly changed the subject. "Shouldn't we be moving on? Places to go, lessons to learn, people to haunt." He attempted a light-hearted smile that looked more like a clown's mug shot.

"Lessons indeed," growled the grumpy spirit, as they flew past the family and out the front door.

"I think the young lad will soon forget all about the regrettable incident in the store and have a delightful time trick-or-treating." Croome tried again. But the cruising carpet supplied the only levity.

This time the airborne time travelers left town entirely and headed out into the countryside where houses were sparse and the trees and fence posts far outnumbered the people. Croome couldn't help but wonder what they were doing so far out in the boonies but didn't dare question the perturbed poltergeist.

Soon, they came to a house festooned with every imaginable type of Halloween light including glowing ghosts, pulsating pumpkins and spurious spiders. Without a moment's hesitation they flew directly at a window that was, technically, closed. Croome instinctively let out a high-pitched yelp and squeezed his eyes shut as he braced for the crashing of glass. When he realized the dreaded impact hadn't happened he gingerly opened his eyes and discovered that they had landed safely inside the house without leaving so much as a smudge on the window.

Once Croome realized that his dignity was the only casualty of their most recent flight, he began to explore their surroundings. He was in a rather ordinary looking room that seemed to be someone's bedroom. He noticed that a nearby bed was nearly covered in a mound of jumbled jackets and crumpled coats.

Gradually, he began to hear noises coming from the next room. Unlike some of their previous destinations, this one was filled with sounds of laughter, levity and light-hearted celebration. The somber Spirit was standing near a closed door and beckoned Croome to follow her as she disappeared through the wooden portal.

Croome, still not accustomed to his apparitional abilities, reached for the doorknob and slowly opened the door. Immediately on the other side was a room full of boisterous young revelers flamboyantly dressed in a wide array of costumes befitting the holiday season. The room was decorated as a haunted house with a wide assortment of creatures hanging from the ceiling and hiding in the corners patiently awaiting their unsuspecting prey. Gruesome monsters snuggled cozily behind each doorway and frozen zombies haunted the various nooks and crannies.

Tumultuous troops of children were bobbing for apples, pinning tales on werewolves and tossing triangular beanbags into wooden Jack-o-lanterns. In a separate room, a group of adults were enjoying beverages that appeared to be off-limits to the younger revelers. Croome noticed one young boy, slightly apart from the others, staring right at him.

"I thought we were invisible to these... these..." Croome struggled for the right word. "... *mortals?*"

"I believe we call them Muggles these days." The Spirit replied, also looking at the young boy. "And we are invisible. But the door that you opened is not invisible. That is why we go through them rather than open them."

Croome felt like a rookie being chastised by a more

experienced phantom. Then he noticed the little boy tugging at the sleeve of one of the adults and pointing toward the mysterious, moving door. The adult glanced to where the boy was pointing and, seeing nothing out of the ordinary, turned back away.

Croome couldn't resist having a little fun. He noticed the little boy still eying the door with suspicion, so he reached out and moved it back and forth. Now the little boy's eyes grew as wide as mini-pumpkins. Croome was starting to enjoy this Halloween thing more with each passing encounter, until he felt a brief jolt of electricity from a bewitching cattle prod and realized that his magical mentor wasn't the least bit amused by his juvenile high-jinx.

Before the Spirit could start lecturing him about not interacting with mortals, Croome asked her a question. "We're out in the middle of nowhere. Where do all of these Halloween partiers come from?" Croome motioned to all the costumed kids and roisterous adults in the adjoining rooms.

"You would be wise to worry less about where they come from, but why they are here." The spirit answered, slightly less peeved than before. "They travel from far and wide to enjoy this festive holiday with like-minded friends. Like so many other holidays, Halloween is about more than just the costumes and candy. It's about the fun and friendship. It is about people finding a reason for getting together and enjoying each other's company." Then the spirit looked toward Croome. "Do you remember fun, Decimus?"

Whether he remembered it or not was unimportant. Whether he had been an active and willing participant was of the utmost importance. And the answer to that question was a definitive no. Decimus Croome had not participated in Halloween or in any other holiday for a very long time. In fact, he had not even participated much in any form of joyful or meaningful pastime for many, many years.

Before Croome had time to dwell on his somber existence, the spirit whisked him away to a very different environment than the rural oasis of their last visit. Soon they were flying over a massively large city. Croome was never much of a city boy and had spent very little time among the bright lights of urban sprawl. He now looked down, in horror, at all the skyscrapers, traffic and bustle. Just when he was thinking how glad he was that they were above it all, the seemingly autonomous flying carpet swooped down, right into the midst of the bustle.

Like some type of military assault jet, they plummeted into the cavernous abyss of skyscrapers, snaking between buildings that seemed to offer very little room for aerobatic error. Once again, Croome found himself wide-eyed and speechless with the exception of an occasional whimper.

Soon, they were soaring over a palatial neighborhood with houses that looked more like mansions than homes. The entire area was surrounded by iron fences and accessed through imposing gates. Despite its enclosure, it was swarming with young trick-or-treaters scampering from door to door and walking away with candy bars the size of bread loaves. Each house was distributing a treasure trove of treats that made the kids squeal with delight. And the homeowners seemed to be just as delighted to see the youngsters so enthusiastic and thankful.

Croome questioned the witchly spirit. "Are they not just showing off their wealth? It is easy for them to be generous when they possess such abundance."

"You are right… and you are wrong. They do indeed have an abundance of wealth, but it's about more than one's ability to give. It's about one's willingness to give. And also," she said, pointing to the nearest resident who had just distributed more of the Halloween treats. "It's about the gift of happiness. These people who have so much cannot buy happiness. But they have discovered that Halloween is the one time they can freely share their abundance and see the joy that it brings, even if only for one night."

"So are you saying that money buys happiness? That happiness is only accessible to those who are wealthy?"

"Aaahh my skeptical friend. I believe it is time for us to move on to our next stop where you may get a chance to answer your own question." With that, they soared into the air and left the opulence behind them.

Their course seemed to take them from the heart of the city to one of the more downtrodden neighborhoods. It was a sharp contrast from the bucolic small town and the remote rural area they had already visited.

Croome wasn't sure what he feared more; continuing their treacherous roller coaster journey through the city skies or stopping in this seemingly perilous neighborhood. Of course he really had no choice. The spirit had an agenda, and they were on a crash-course to complete it.

This time, instead of going inside the houses, they stopped on the outside of one just as a motley band of trick-or-treaters came to the door. Each of the young urchins was dressed in a costume, but none of them were costumes that Croome recognized. It was if they had been thrown together from odds and ends lying about their homes. Some wore their regular tattered clothing with only shabby old masks for a costume. Others had no mask at all but were wearing clothes representing some cultural icon of which Croome was completely ignorant. Despite their disparate appearance, the group was in high spirits and laughed enthusiastically as they knocked on the door of the nearest house.

The burley resident who answered the door smiled broadly when the kids chanted their trick-or-treats. Despite the cold weather, he wore a sleeveless shirt that revealed a large tattoo on his even larger biceps. His gap-toothed grin was not diminished in the least by his rough-hewn exterior. He didn't seem to understand what the kids were saying, but he fully understood and appreciated the universal language of Halloween. He handed out one small treat per child and tried valiantly to apologize for his meager allotment of Halloween delicacies. The kids didn't seem to mind in the least and all were quite thankful for each treat that was doled out.

Croome watched the scene in fascination. It was obvious that the resident of this particular home lived a meager lifestyle. Yet somehow he managed to provide treats, paltry as they were, for the children. And his interactions with these costumed visitors seemed to bring abundant joy to the man. It was almost as if the trick-or-treaters and their benefactor had some sort of symbiotic relationship, each providing essential benefits to the other.

Croome was fascinated at the interactions that unfolded beneath him. "How can one with so little give so much?"

The spirit turned toward Croome. "Who is giving and who is receiving?" She asked, with absolutely none of her usual wit and whimsy.

Croome, realizing he was not exactly an expert on the subject of Halloween largesse, feebly tried to demonstrate that he had learned his lesson. "I may not have fully realized the joy of Halloween in the past, but you have shown me the true spirit of the holiday. From this point on,

I am a changed man. I will always hold these lessons in my heart."

"Will you?" Was all the spirit had to say. Obviously she was unimpressed by Croome's newfound change of heart. Without further comment, she directed Croome back onto their floating ferry.

"We have two more stops." She indicated. Croome realized that she was no longer as mischievous and merry as before. It was probably his imagination, but Croome noticed that his companion seemed to be fading in both spirit and appearance. It was as if she were gradually diminishing with each stop, withering with each lesson she imparted upon her apprehensive apprentice.

On their soaring journey back home, Croome pondered what he had witnessed throughout this enlightening evening. Was this his legacy or his destiny? Did the lessons he learned on this memorable Halloween actually cause meaningful change or was he doomed to be a grumbling grouch until the end of his years? He desperately wanted to be a better person but wondered if it was truly possible for someone to significantly change their lifelong outlook.

As Croome raced headlong through the heavens, his

mind ponderously plodded over these thoughts and so many more. The next thing he knew, they were hovering over Casa de Croome. A group of trick-or-treaters was just walking up the sidewalk toward his front door completely unaware, as they innocently knocked on the door, that they were about to encounter the Grouch Who Stole Halloween. As soon as the door opened, the airborne Croome came face to face with the terrestrial Croome who looked noticeably less joyful than the previous Halloween greeters they had just visited.

They slipped silently past the gloomy Croome and settled in his living room within earshot of the nearby Halloween interactions. They heard the ubiquitous shouts of "trick-or-treat" from the children and the much less joyful sound of Croome's growling response. "Enough of your trick-or-treating. What you really mean is give us a bribe or we'll vandalize your house. Now take this and get along to your next crime scene." With that, Decimus Croome tossed exactly one carrot stick into each treat bag. The previously happy Halloweeners were suddenly silent with the exception of a couple dispirited thank-yous.

The visiting Croome objected. "This is the old me. I

swear I have changed. If I could grab this mean-spirited fellow by the collar and shake some sense into him, I would do it in a heartbeat. He has not seen what I have seen. He is still the curmudgeon Croome of yesterday. He is not the enlightened Croome who stands before you."

The rapidly fading spirit motioned toward the door indicating that Croome was sentenced to continue witnessing the scene that was about to transpire. Croome reluctantly looked on as one poor band of young trick-or-treaters after another was disheartened with meager tidbits and overly generous verbal abuse.

"You call that a costume?" Croome said to one young visitor whose spirited smile quickly turned into a puzzled frown.

The next guest was greeted with, "Shouldn't you be home doing homework?"

The insults only worsened as dusk turned to dark, right along with Croome's blasphemous behavior.

Croome continued to disgrace... "Are you supposed to be scary or just plain ugly?"

...and scorn... "Aren't you too old to be trick-or-treating?"

…and taunt…"Didn't your parents teach you not to beg?"

…and shame. "I don't give to the panderers on street corners. Why should I encourage the ones trespassing at my doorstep?"

No phantom was more haunting, no demon more daunting than the callous Croome and his slanderous slams upon the unsuspecting and undeserving young hobgoblins who visited him upon that evening. Each insult was nastier than the one before as minute by minute, the marauding malcontent managed to change the mood from merriment and mirth to malice and malevolence. Rather than the symbiotic feeling of joy and fulfillment that usually accompanied the trick-or-treating ritual, Croome was now witnessing the equivalent of a verbal massacre, and he could take no more.

"Enough." He whispered, hanging his head in shame.

"Not enough." Returned the spirit in a solemn voice. "We have yet one more stop before I release you to your next and final visitor of the evening."

While Croome pondered his malicious past, the duo joylessly journeyed from Croome's house to his daughter's amply decorated home where lights streamed from all the windows and the atmosphere was decidedly different than the dour dwelling they had just visited. Inside, the mood and activities were similar to the rural house they had witnessed earlier. Only this house had nearly twice as many people of all shapes, sizes and ages; and Croome recognized most of them.

The first person he encountered was his sister dressed up like a vampiress and his brother-in-law looking every bit like the famed Count Dracula. His own grandson, the same one who had recently visited him at the hardware store, was dressed as a western cowboy complete with felt chaps, faux-leather holsters and plastic guns, more mild west than wild west. Croome continued to scan the room and saw neighbors, customers and other folks he hadn't seen in years.

Croome still hadn't seen the party hosts, his daughter and son-in-law. Just as he was about to search for them, in walked Sam Bobbich and his family with little Tommy in a pretty impressive Popeye costume, standing between his two proud parents who were dressed a little less convincingly as Brutus and Olive Oyl. Kate Bobbich trailed closely behind dressed as some pop diva. Croome beamed with delight when he saw The Bobbich clan. He was relieved that his daughter treated them with kindness, even though her father had been a complete ogre to them.

And Eve wasn't the only one with Halloween spirit. Croome watched as one party guest after another complimented Tommy on his costume. Even the youngsters who had never heard of Popeye crowded around him and treated him like royalty. They all loved Tommy's costume, even though many of them were a bit puzzled about who his parents were supposed to be.

After a while Tommy got tired of explaining who Brutus and Olive Oyl were and just began making up creative stories. He told some people they were bible characters and others that they were Greek gods. He had the most fun telling other kids that they were celebrities named Sonny and Cher.

As Croome looked on, he noticed the lively young Tommy began to slow down. Even his ever-present smile became more labored as the evening progressed. His shining eyes gradually lost their luster and, at one point, it looked as if he was about to fall asleep. Even worse, it was obvious that something was bothering him; his skin was nearly as pale as the make-up on Croome's brother-in-law the Count.

"Is the boy going to be alright?" Croome asked, nodding in Tommy's direction.

When he got no reply from the Spirit, Croome turned his attention back to young Tommy. He noticed that the boy not only looked like his father but he also seemed to inherit his father's selflessness. Croome watched closely as the boy's eyelids seemed to grow heavy and his gait grew slower. Yet he kept smiling through it all, determined not to spoil the party for anyone else.

But of course his parents were also watching Tommy closely and continued to exchange concerned glances with one another. Even young Kate was beginning to drop hints that it might be time for her brother to hit the hay. They all knew how much Tommy loved Halloween parties, but they also knew how tired he got, from both the chemotherapy and the leukemia itself. Between the trick-or-treating and the party, he was definitely slowing down. With great reluctance, they made their way toward their son.

"It's time to go Tommy." His mom gently reminded

him. "You have had a busy day at school and out trick-or-treating. Let's thank the Tates for inviting us and then head home." Tommy was obviously disappointed to be leaving but put up only the feeblest attempts to resist. He was every bit as tired as he looked.

Before the Bobbiches left, Eve Tate insisted on handing out the Dracademy Awards, evidently a tradition from previous Halloween parties. Very few party attendees escaped the ceremony without some sort of award, so they usually dragged on for quite a while. But Eve could see that Tommy was waning fast, so she shuffled the Bobbich family awards to the top of the stack.

After rounding up every beast, goblin, superhero and dastardly villain in the house, Eve got started with the ceremony. "We have a tie for the Most Confusing Costume award." Most people in the room already knew whom the award recipients would be and looked in the direction of Sam and Belinda Bobbich.

Eve continued, "I'm not sure who to give this award to though. When I tallied the votes, half of you voted for Brutus and Olive Oyl and half of you voted for Sonny and Cher."

Accompanied by raucous laughter and cheering, Sam and Belinda Bobbich strolled up to accept the award, and Belinda gave the obligatory acceptance speech. "We'd like to thank our son Tommy for confusing all of you. Without his help, we'd have never won this award."

To a chorus of cheers and applause, Eve Tate retrieved the microphone from Belinda. "Speaking of Tommy, the next award is the prestigious Best Costume of the Year. This is our biggest prize of the night and was a hands-down, unanimous winner. Ladies and gentlemen, this year's Best Costume Award goes to Popeye the Sailor Man played by the strong and handsome Tommy Bobbich."

The thundering applause and heartfelt congratulations seemed to revive Tommy better than any medicine or medical treatments known to mankind, and he shyly but happily accepted his award with a smile that spread throughout the room. Long after the Bobbich family departed the Halloween festivities, they were the talk of the town, and it was obvious that they would not have to face their upcoming struggles alone.

Croome, who had been silently observing recent events finally found the words to describe what he had seen and felt. "Everyone is so caring and helpful."

"Everyone?" Asked the spirit.

Croome didn't have to answer the question. For at that very moment he noticed his daughter, Eve, and grandson, Kellen, stood nearby. Kellen's hair was dripping wet after a recent apple-bobbing competition. Eve was towel-drying Kellen's head while he chattered on about his successful bid to free the elusive apples from the tub of water. Then, with barely a breath between sentences, he changed topics. "Why doesn't Grandpa Croome come to our parties? The only time I ever see him is at the store."

Croome's daughter wiped a strand of wet hair from the boy's forehead and got a serious look on her face. "Do you remember the Christmas show about the Grinch?"

Kellen laughed as he thought about his favorite holiday movie. "He stole Christmas from Whoville."

"He certainly tried to, didn't he?" Kellen's mom smiled as she continued. "Sometimes your Grandpa Croome reminds me of the Grinch. He's just not a big fan of the holidays and seems almost as if he doesn't like to see other people enjoying them either."

Upon hearing this Croome went pale and let out an

involuntary moan. For the first time, he saw how others perceived him, and it was especially painful to hear the scathing critique from his own daughter. At the same time, he realized it was true. He had ruined many a Halloween through his obstinate crankiness.

"Was Grandpa Croome a Halloween Grinch when you were a little girl, too?"

"I'm afraid I don't really remember him ever being much of a Halloween fan. But I'm told that he loved Halloween at one time. Before your grandma…" she paused. "…went away."

The young lad pondered this, and then said. "I wish Grampa was here. I want to show him my costume. Maybe we can go trick-or-treat at his house." Eve Tate glanced at her husband who quickly jumped into the conversation.

"I'm not sure your Grampa Croome is home right now." He didn't realize how true that statement was.

Kellen didn't seem too concerned one way or the other and with a quick, "Okay!" he ran off to join his costumed friends.

Darren Tate noticed the crestfallen look on his wife's face. "It's okay honey. You can't expect to change your father. He's made his decisions and nothing we can say or do will make a difference."

"But he's missing out on so much. They are both missing out on so much. Kellen will only be a kid for a little while longer. He'll only be a little Halloween goblin for a couple more years."

Her husband wrapped her in his arms and pulled her close. "I wish I knew what to tell you. He is what he is, and you're absolutely right. He's missing out on so much. And Kellen would love to have a grandfather, even if only for the holidays."

"I can't help but wonder what it would be like if Mom was here instead of Dad. Is it terrible of me to think that way about my own father?"

"Your father has decided how he wants to live his life, and you have decided how you want to live yours. You can't let his choices ruin your Halloween every year."

Old Decimus Croome could take no more. "I have seen enough spirit. I beg of you, release me from this nightmare. Please let me go back to my pitiful life so that I can change my miserable ways."

"I will indeed release you, for my time with you has

expired. But you are not free to slumber. For you have yet to meet some very important visitors." Croome had grown weary to the point of near paralysis. His mind was completely dominated by an odd mixture of shame and self-pity. He had some vague sense of curiosity as to what the witch meant by 'visitors.' According to his calculations, he had only to endure one last visit with one last spirit. But he was in no frame of mind to care about or decipher any more riddles.

---

Croome had no recollection of how he got home. He remembered no wild carpet ride, no bracing autumn air and no sweeping vistas. One minute he was at his daughter's house and the next minute he was at his own home, in his own bedroom.

Croome looked intently at the witch who seemed to have faded even more. "Please spirit. Before you depart, are the visions that I have already seen and are about to see what will inevitably happen or what might happen? Am I doomed to be the wretched creature that we just witnessed?

Am I doomed to inflict misery on all those that I encounter?"

It appeared as if the Ghost of Halloween Present was about to fade away to oblivion either refusing or unable to answer Croome's pitiful question. But some small whisper of a movement caught his attention and Croome's eyes became transfixed upon the spot where the witch's robe met the floor. To his horror and dismay, he saw two hideous little heads pop out from under the garments. He quickly stepped back, frightened by what he saw, uncertain of what it was he perceived.

The witch seemed to be morbidly entertained by the look of fear and disgust on Croome's face. "I see you have met my two little friends." She said, looking down upon the gruesome looking creatures.

"What are they and why do you keep them hidden beneath your black robes?" Croome cringed, backing further away. "Do these abominable little monsters belong to you?"

"Yes and no. They are mine, they are yours, they are ours. They belong to all of us and none of us. They are children of the world. They are old and they are new, but they have grown particularly repulsive in the present day."

"You speak in riddles. What are these horrible hobgoblins you keep hidden from view?"

The witch smiled, a feeble yet somewhat vexing smile. "Let me introduce you to Apathy and Greed. When I am long gone, they will remain to haunt you and your brethren. Like children, they appear small but have a remarkable impact upon us all."

"But why are they here with you?"

The witch let out a particularly revolting cackle that ended in a feeble, sickly cough. At the same time, the two young beasts emerged from under her robes, their tiny gnarled limbs sticking through their tattered clothing. "They are not here with me, Decimus Croome. They are here with you."

And with that, the two beasts advanced upon Croome as if to devour him with their jagged teeth and to claw at him with their deformed limbs. Croome let out a screech and instinctively backed away. As he did so, the witch disappeared while the two creatures remained, bearing down on him with frightening speed.

"No. No!!!" Croome cried out, putting his arms up in

front of his face as if to fend off the impending doom.

# Chapter 11 - The Spirit of Halloween Future

"No, no!!! Keep these horrible creatures away from me." Croome thrashed around in his bed before waking in a terrible fright. His sheets and blankets clung to his sweat-drenched skin as he looked around to see…

…absolutely no one. He was wide-awake and shivering both from fright and from the cold draft on his dampened body.

Sitting upright, he began to mutter into his lap. "One more. One more Halloween spirit. I'm not sure if I can take one more reminder of what a fool I have been. What a selfish, greedy old fool."

"Oh Spirit of the Future," Croome cried out into his empty bedchamber. "I have learned my lesson. I realize that I was a cold and cantankerous human being. But I will change. I promise I will change. You do not need to visit me as your two fellow Spirits have done. They have taught me all I need to know. From now on, I will be a changed man. I will be a better man."

All was silent in the room. For a moment Croome

thought that maybe the final Specter would not make his apocalyptic house call, and he breathed easier. In fact, he dropped his face into his huge hands and began to sob. So many emotions poured over him, drowning him in torrents of regret and shame. He sat for what felt like hours drenching his own meaty palms in the tears of lamentation, feeling the tremendous weight of a lifetime of selfish misdeeds and neglect.

At first he didn't notice the marked chill that enshrouded the room. It wasn't until he raised his head and saw his own frosty breath rolling off his lips that he realized something was amiss.

Then through a cloudy veil of frosty breath and tears, he saw a gray-black shadow drifting over the floor toward him. At first he thought it was his own blurred vision and nothing more. But as he wiped away the tears, he saw the apparition begin to take on a more distinct form as it drew near.

Now Croome could see that he was being approached by a true phantasm that was less distinct yet more frightening than the previous spirits. Its form seemed to ebb and flow, to shimmer and solidify revealing three distinct yet indistinct layers. The outside layer consisted of a dark albeit transparent cloak that ran from the neck to below the feet. Underneath that semi-transparent layer was the faint outline of a long and lanky body that was as fluid as the river Styx. And finally, under its ghastly pale epidermis lay a skeletal structure that seemed to hold it all together. Each bone danced about beneath the other two layers as the spirit slithered along the floor toward Croome.

Croome knew at once that he was witnessing the final spirit to visit him. He knew, but the knowing did nothing to allay his fears. This final Spirit would not be as congenial as the previous ones; Croome knew this instinctively and assuredly. And the dire thought made him want to bury his head back into his capacious palms and shield himself from the impending onslaught.

That is what he wanted to do, but that is not what he did. For at once, he realized that what he had already witnessed on this evening and what he was about to witness was a product of his own deplorable decisions. He had built a wall around himself and blocked out everyone and everything that might possibly cause him harm. And in the process, he had been the one to cause untold damage to all those whose lives he touched.

So Croome stood up from his rumpled bed and faced the oncoming specter. His legs were weak, his hands were trembling, but his voice was surprisingly steady. "Welcome Spirit of Halloweens to Come. I fear what you are about to show me, but I stand ready to follow you wherever you may lead and to learn what you are about to teach me."

The specter now rose to its full height in front of Croome. At first Croome could only see darkness under its hooded cowl. It appeared empty and black as the darkest caverns of hell. But then two glowing orbs peered out of the darkness. Two eyes that flickered like candles and shone like burning coal seemed to fixate on Croome and peer into his soul. Frightened but resolute, Croome stood his ground and waited for direction from the Spirit.

The direction did not come in the form of words, for the Spirit was silent. Instead it raised one spectral finger and motioned for Croome to follow as it turned away and flowed noiselessly toward the open window of the bedroom. As the spirit drifted away, its already ethereal form seemed to melt into a cloudy trail of obscurity. And it was on just such a cloudy trail that Croome now started drifting as if being pulled along by the nebulous gravity of this most mysterious of all spirits.

Once again, they floated over the neighboring houses and toward the center of town and, once again, ended up on Main Street. Nothing appeared to have changed until they arrived at the old family hardware store. Croome immediately noticed the absence of the big Croome's Hardware sign out front. Instead he saw large white letters painted across the store's windows spelling out the words "GOING OUT OF BUSINESS SALE" and "ALL ITEMS PRICED TO SELL."

Croome was shocked to see how barren and ugly the old store looked. He couldn't help but remember the flower boxes and meticulous displays that always adorned the windows when his father ran the store. Now, in addition to Decimus's years of neglect, the store looked vacant and forlorn.

But as they grew nearer, Croome was relieved to see intermittent customers entering and leaving the store. The ones who were leaving appeared to be carrying bags of merchandise. Croome recognized some of the shoppers as customers he hadn't seen in years, decades in some cases.

The spirit, followed by Croome, soared into the store, and a scene of chaos immediately confronted them. One half of the store was a jumble of shelves and merchandise that appeared to have little rhyme nor reason. Plumbing supplies were heaped together with electrical gewgaws and tools were scattered with absolutely no semblance of order. The other half of the store was barren and cordoned off with orange plastic ribbon as if it was a forbidden crime scene.

Scanning the barely recognizable store, Croome realized that there was a thematic structure after all. One shelf was labeled 60% off, one was 70% off, another was 80% off, and one even carried a 90% off sign. And around each shelf and table swarmed a mass of shoppers looking every bit like ants scurrying around a drop of honey.

Even the people seemed to be divided into two groups. The most frantic group seemed intent on amassing as many sale items as possible and getting out of the store as quickly as possible. Croome recognized few of these shoppers and realized that many of them were from nearby towns.

The other group was mostly locals, and they were as interested in conversation as they were in shopping. It was to this knot of humanity that the voiceless spirit pointed as if directing Croome to join their intense discussion. Croome drew near the group and began to hear snatches of their conversation.

"I never thought I'd see this place again. It's been years since I've been in here." This from a largish gentleman who was inspecting one of the items on the 70% Off table. "*Old Gloomy Croome* would roll over in his grave if he saw his precious merchandise being sold for these prices."

"Hell, I might have come in here more often if he would have sold stuff for this cheap." Another customer, who looked familiar to Croome, exclaimed. He was having trouble concentrating on the 70% off items when the 80% ones seemed to beckon him with a magnetic pull.

The portly gentleman set down the item he was examining and was also drawn toward the more generous sale. "Are you kidding? I wouldn't have come in here even if he gave this stuff away. *Gloomy Croome* used to yell at my kids every time they'd pick up something. The only thing Croome hated worse than customers was customers' kids."

"He was a cranky old fart." the second shopper agreed. "I always felt like I needed to apologize for shopping in his store."

Just then a jolly woman, even larger than her hefty husband, joined the conversation. "I don't think anyone will miss that old skinflint. But I remember when his dad ran the store. Back then it was fun to shop here even when we didn't buy anything. Sweet old Stan Croome was the friendliest businessman in town. I especially liked coming in here when I was a little girl..." She continued, seeming to be lost in her reminiscence.

While Croome struggled to imagine the lady as a little girl, his mind grew hazy and his vision cloudy. Gradually the current scene faded away and was replaced by a vision of the store from many years ago, back when Decimus was still a teenager. His father was talking and laughing with one customer while others browsed the neat and tidy shelves of the store. One customer approached him asking for advice about a plumbing problem while another hovered nearby, waiting for his turn to speak with the congenial Stan Croome. It was almost as if they were school children lined up to speak with their favorite teacher.

The vision slowly faded away and the three customers

were still discussing their memories of the store. "Do you remember what Decimus Croome used to say when you asked him to help you find something in the store?"

"How could I forget? It was about the only thing he ever said to anyone. 'If you can't find it, then we probably don't have it.'"

The group laughed and the lady added, "Then he walked away like you had some kind of contagious disease." More laughter as they wandered to the next sale table.

"Didn't Croome have a daughter?" The lady asked while rummaging through a badly jumbled pile of hardware. "I wonder why she didn't take over the store like *Gloomy Croome* did from his dad?"

"Croomey inherited the store because he worked with his dad." One of the other locals said. "Do you think his daughter would have wanted to work with him?"

"Nobody would want to work with Croome."

"Speaking of working with Croome, what ever happened to that nice Sam Bobbich man? He was the only thing in this store with a personality."

"I haven't seen him since his poor little son..."

"I heard about that. That was about the same time old

Croome..."

"Poor Sam. To lose both his job and his..."

"Let's not talk about this anymore. There won't be anything left on the 90% off table if we don't get over there."

The trio departed leaving Decimus Croome frustrated and curious. He looked at the spirit. "What were they talking about? What happened to little Tommy? And why did Sam lose his job? I wasn't very friendly, but I never would have fired him. He was the only one who could keep inventory on that blasted computer and," Croome hesitated. "And I liked him. He was the only person I ever really talked to."

Croome realized how absurd he sounded. He didn't even talk much to Sam Bobbich. Come to think of it, he didn't really talk much to anyone.

Without warning, the Spirit began to float away, pulling Croome along in his wake. Croome didn't argue or complain. He felt rather numb and powerless. He knew he would get no answer, but he asked anyway. "Where are you taking me, Spirit? I have seen enough to realize what a fool I have been. What else could you possibly show me?"

Croome knew he would get no answer. He also knew that an answer wasn't necessary for soon he would find out their fated destination. Although he had a strong hunch that he knew precisely where they were going. So he followed in the shadow of a shadow trying to recall the conversations he had just heard.

Soon, Croome realized that his hunch had been absolutely correct. For below them, in the same neighborhood where his daughter lived, was the Bobbich home. It was a modest house, small and simple. As expected Sam and his wife kept the place neat and tidy, and the yard was neatly manicured with a row of shrubs around the perimeter and tiny gardens dotted here and there around the meticulously landscaped property.

Croome hoped to see little Tommy Bobbich playing in the yard but was not surprised to see otherwise. Despite its well-kept appearance, the house had an aura of gloom about it that no amount of flowers or sunshine could dispel.

As the spirit gently touched down near the front steps of the Bobbich house, Croome was relieved to see young Kate Bobbich walking out the front door. The first thing he noticed was how much she seemed to have aged since the last time he saw her in the Home Emporium store. He also realized that she was carrying a large cardboard box and was walking toward a dusty yellow moving van parked in the driveway.

Once Kate had walked down the front steps, Croome spied a large sign posted on the front screen door with the word "**FORECLOSURE**" scrawled across the top in bold, black print. Below that, in slightly smaller red letters, were the words "Public Auction."

Croome struggled to digest the meaning of such an ominous sign. He was even more perplexed by the date written at the very bottom of the sign. It was exactly one year into the future.

The spirit slowly flowed into the house like an irritable stream of lava flowing down the side of a fiery volcano. Croome had little choice but to follow. It was a small house and, of course, Croome had never set foot inside it before. He assumed it was never much of a palace considering the meager wages he paid Sam. But it looked especially barren to the two hovering visitors.

Bare shelves sat below desolate cupboards while empty

drawers jutted out in between. Croome felt depressed as he drifted through the bleak kitchen and into the adjoining dining room where Sam and Belinda sat at a small, round table, deep in discussion.

In the middle of the table sat a pile of family treasures. Most of the baubles looked insignificant to Croome, but Belinda Bobbich thought otherwise. Both of her hands rested on top of a well-worn game box as if she was guarding it from marauding thieves. "But we can't leave this behind. It was Tommy's favorite game. He wanted to play this every day when he was a little boy."

Sam smiled at his wife over the mound of family heirlooms. "Tommy loved to play games, didn't he?" Now he moved his hand to rest on top of the box also, right beside Belinda's. "And he didn't even care if he won or not. He just loved being with his family, no matter what we were doing."

Belinda moved her hand so that her extended index finger touched her husband's. "Can't we please at least keep this one game? Every time I look at it, I think of Tommy."

Just then Kate walked back in the house and overheard her parents' conversation. "We can't get rid of *Pirate's*

*Treasure*! That was Tommy's favorite!"

Sam smiled weakly as he glanced from his wife to his daughter. "We can keep *Pirate's Treasure*." Now his glance shifted toward the stack of disputed keepsakes in the middle of the table. "I wish we could keep everything. But we won't have room for it all in the apartment."

Sam's mention of the new apartment seemed to put a dampening chill in the air. There was a dismal silence that seemed to drain all life out of the room until Kate wistfully questioned her parents. "Do we have to move? This is the only house I've ever known. This is where Tommy and I…"

Sam hesitantly interrupted his daughter. "We've discussed this Kate. We don't own this house any more." He couldn't face either of the women in his life as he choked on the words. "The bank owns it now." Then, in a voice that was barely audible, "We have to leave this house and move into our new apartment."

Belinda Bobbich, seemingly oblivious to the conversation between her husband and daughter, began to absently sort through some of the smaller items on the table. She gently picked up one of Tommy's favorite picture books and began slowly leafing through the pages. "First we lose Tommy." She stopped at each page, savoring the memories of evenings spent reading the books aloud to her children. "Now we lose our house."

Kate stretched out her arm to gently grasp her mother's hand. "We'll be okay Mom."

"Maybe we can buy another house some day." Sam's voice was subdued as he tried to reassure his wife and daughter. "Once we pay off some of the medical bills."

Belinda seemed as if she hadn't heard her husband. Still holding Kate with one hand, she picked up Tommy's toy hammer with the other. As if the plastic tool reminded her of Sam's job, her gaze turned from reflective to bitter. "None of this would have happened if it wasn't for that miserly old skinflint Decimus Croome."

Kate and Sam glanced at one another. They both knew how Belinda felt about her husband's stingy boss. Sam tried to avert the oncoming tirade. "I understand how you feel honey; but we can't blame everything on Mr. Croome. I don't think he even realized how sick Tommy was. Maybe, if I would have told him, he would have given me…"

"Croome wouldn't have given you a drink of water if he

was drowning in it." Her voice took on the sharpened edge of both anger and pain. "He was a bitter old man who only cared about himself. He didn't care about you; he didn't care about me." Belinda's voice cracked, and she was barely able to finish speaking. "And he didn't care about our little Tommy. That man didn't care about anything but money."

Sam slowly stood and walked around the table to where his wife was sitting. He gently placed his hand on her shoulder while grasping Kate's hand in his other. "There, there my darling. You are most likely right. But we can't speak badly of Mr. Croome. He provided me with a job so that we could have food on our table."

"A job?" Belinda's voice rose from sorrow to anger. "You call that a job? He barely paid you enough to survive. And he treated you like a slave rather than an employee. It was because of Croome that we couldn't get Tommy the help he needed. It was because of Croome that we lost our house. It was because of Croome that we couldn't take Tommy to a decent hospital. It was because of Croome..." Belinda began pounding her fists on the table.

Sam gently caressed his wife's neck and shoulders. "None of that matters any more, sweetheart. Tommy's gone." Sam gently kissed his wife on the top of her head. "And Mr. Croome's gone too."

"Our Tommy would still be here if Croome had left long ago. You could have worked anywhere. Why did you work for that dreadful man?"

Sam Bobbich sat for a moment in silence. He seemed to be deciding whether to answer the question or overlook it as he had for so many years. "You probably don't remember Mr. Croome's father, Stan, do you?" He didn't wait for a reply as he thought back to his childhood. "One of my first memories was visiting Croome's Hardware store with my dad. We went there a lot, because my dad was always working on our house or yard and always needed to buy screws, bolts, nails, lumber and anything else you can imagine. But I don't think he just went in to get supplies. I think he liked visiting with Stan Croome as much as I did. Old Stan was always pleasant and helpful." He didn't say it, but it hung in the air. Sam remembered Stan Croome as being the opposite of his son, Decimus.

"I always wanted to work at Croome's Hardware. Ever since I was a little kid. I just felt welcome and glad every time I went in there. Then when we got married, it seemed like a good job. I wish Mr. Croome had been a bit more like his father. But I needed the job, and we wanted to stay here in Timberton. Then Kate came along, then Tommy…" Sam's voice trailed off to silence.

Croome could take no more. He knelt directly in front of kind Sam Bobbich and began pleading. "Sam, Sam. I was such a fool. I am so sorry. Why didn't I realize what a good father you were? What a good friend you were. I treated you so horribly. I treated everyone horribly, but especially you. If I could go back and change things I would. If I could bring back little Tommy, I would. Please hear me Sam. Please forgive me. I beg of you, Sam."

Sam was unfazed by Croome's pleas because he was oblivious to them. Croome turned to the Spirit in desperation. "Oh Spirit why can't he hear me? How can I make myself heard by this kind man I have treated so poorly? How can I ever apologize to him and make him understand that I have changed? How can I tell him that I would gladly go back in time and withdraw every cruel word I ever said if only I could?"

Only silence. Cold, dead silence.

"You say nothing spirit, yet I hear every word you do

not say. Your silence clearly shows me what a fool I have been. So why then can't Sam hear my miserable begging and heartfelt pleading?"

Croome continued beseeching the silent Spirit. "If he cannot hear me in this spiritual form, is it too late for the real Croome to help him? Is it too late for me to make amends to all the people I have hurt with my shameful words and actions?"

Not a word from the stone-faced Spirit as it once more reached out a cold and shimmering hand toward Decimus Croome. Croome grasped the shadowy fingers and could feel that the Spirit was beginning to lose strength. It was beginning to lose substance and was subtly, almost imperceptibly, beginning to fade into oblivion, as had the previous Spirits.

Once again Croome found himself being helplessly conveyed to a new time and place. This time he was spirited away to the outskirts of town, to a place he had only visited once before. It was a place that brought back painful memories of a time long ago when his life dreadfully spiraled downward into a bottomless pit of despair.

It was not a place Croome wanted to visit. In fact it was a place he had determined never again to visit after his last agonizing journey here. "Please Spirit. Anyplace but here." Croome pleaded. "I have sworn never to return to this land of malignant memories."

Paying no heed to Croome's entreaties, the Spirit continued through the open gates and into the garden of neatly planted tombstones. The first thing Croome noticed was the freshly tilled soil of a recently planted resident. He was careful not to look at the engraved granite for fear of seeing the name 'Tommy Bobbich' etched permanently thereon.

Nor did he desire to see the name of his beloved Patricia nor the hallowed ground in which she lay reposed forever in sleepless rest. Yet that was exactly where the Spirit was leading him.

Croome moaned, "Please Spirit. This is a lesson I have learned well and do not need a refresher course. I vowed never to visit here again to relive the worst days of my life. Nothing you show me here will teach me a lesson I have not already learned."

As they grew closer, Croome could read the one and

only biography he had ever written. It was composed of few letters and even fewer words yet spoke a truth that transcended all other words he had ever written or spoken.

Here Lies

Patricia Croome

Beloved Wife & Mother

The Light of Our Lives

Gone But Never Forgotten

It was a death poem, the hardest words Croome had ever written, so revealing, yet so insufficient. So truthful yet so harsh. So fleeting, yet so permanent. Croome wanted to fly from this field of sorrow with its harsh memories and poignant reminders. He was relieved as the Spirit led him away, yet surprised to see a similar tombstone nearby. It was the exact same size, shape and color. But the wording on it was equally revealing in its brevity. Croome stopped short, an involuntary groan escaping his ghostly pale lips.

Here Lies

Decimus Croome

A hundred, no a thousand cruel words could not have spoken more accurately nor more eloquently than all the words that were not included on this permanent and stark epitaph. The words that spoke most vividly of Croome's life were the missing words on his final chapter written so succinctly in stone.

Turning to the Spirit, Croome fell to his knees and grasped for the ethereal robes of the silent sentinel. "Please!!" He cried out, grasping at thin air. "This cannot be how it ends. Please tell me that this is not final. Please tell me that I still have a chance to make amends for the cruel and heartless life I have lived."

The Spirit replied in the same fashion he had replied upon previous occasions. Eternal silence.

Croome bent over the cold slab of stone that bore his name. He beat his fists upon the hard, gray surface and pleaded forgiveness. As if in answer to his entreaty, a gnarled and bedraggled black cat emerged from behind the stone and slowly curled around the base of the slab and then at the feet of Decimus Croome. When the pathetic animal looked up, Croome could see that it was grievously wounded and malnourished. Despite the drastic and disheveled appearance, Croome knew at once that he was looking at Black Magic, the poor cat who had been his only friend for these past miserable years.

The cat looked up at him with pathetic eyes and shameful disdain. Croome bent over to pet the disheveled animal but was greeted with a loud hiss and a quick swipe of extended claws. The cat arched its back and bared its sharp teeth or what was left of them.

Croome stepped backward and was abruptly stopped by the granite slab of his own headstone. The cat released one last malevolent hiss then limped away without looking back.

"Does no one or nothing mourn my passing?" Croome pathetically implored the Spirit. "Was there no man or animal that felt sorrow upon my death?"

Croome expected no reply so was surprised to see the spirit raise a skeletal hand and spin it about in the air. As if on cue, a small whirlwind of leaves swirled in a spiraling pattern toward Croome. As it reached him, it circled round and round him, then halted as abruptly as it had started. The twirling twister of leaves fell to the ground at his feet with the exception of one large and colorful leaf that came to rest atop his own apocryphal tombstone.

Croome plucked the leaf off the stone and examined it

as if looking for answers on its weathered surface. He looked from the single leaf to the scattered leaves all around him. Then he looked back at the one single leaf and noticed something that had escaped him all these years when he had been too busy to take notice of autumn leaves.

By itself, the leaf looked as old and lackluster as Croome himself. Yet the entire cavalcade of leaves brilliantly blanketed the landscape like a stunning evening dress on a beautiful princess. Croome closely examined the brittle and browning leaf again, then held it at arm's length. Just like the first Spirit that had visited him on this eventful evening, it took him back to kaleidoscopic autumns of yesteryear and reminded him of the joy he received from similar colorful leaves. He saw leaves sandwiched between layers of waxed paper and pressed between the pages of voluminous books, later given to a grateful mother who, for all the world, received the gift as if being presented with a valuable treasure beyond compare.

He saw leaves flattened onto plain white paper and traced with a careful hand and clumsy pencil. Then he saw the traced outline colored to completion by a youthful hand with an orange color crayon. Then the resulting artwork was displayed on a classroom window like paintings hanging in the Louvre and admired by an audience with a much greater appreciation.

And what about the hoards of fallen leaves raked into a ragged mound by father and child only to be redistributed by a cavalcade of flying youth burrowing deep into the sweet-scented pile of delightful detritus? Could any toys crafted by the hands of mankind bring such joy and wonder as this simple leaf, created en masse by Mother Nature?

The Spirit reached out a hand that seemed as thin and brittle as the scrawny branches from which the leaves had fallen. Now Croome was hesitant to leave. He took one last look around, from the leaves on the ground to the headstones that sprouted all around him. Suddenly he wanted to read every last one and feed off the accumulated stories of each individual stone and the accumulated stories of a community. He had spent the last decades looking inward and missed the drama and majesty that had unfolded while he was wrapped up in his own suffocating cocoon of austerity.

He had missed the joy of raising a beautiful daughter, the excitement of watching a community evolve around him and the rewards of sharing in the daily interactions that had presented themselves to him while he stubbornly chose to ridicule and ignore them. With those thoughts, the Spirit bore him toward his home. What would he find when he got there?

A silly question really. Of course he would find an empty house with forgotten hopes and squandered dreams. It was the garden that he had sown for so many years, and it was now harvesting a bountiful crop of sorrow and shame.

The silence of Croome surpassed that of the Spirit as they set down inside a hollow house. Darkness surrounded them, darkness engulfed them and darkness filled them from within. And, like the whirlwind of autumn leaves, the spirit spun around Croome three times then disappeared into the infinite darkness leaving Croome alone with his melancholy memories.

# Chapter 12 - A Very Croomey Halloween

Croome noticed a scrap on the floor at the exact spot where the Spirit had disappeared. Bending over, he picked it up and realized it was not a scrap at all but a fragile autumn leaf. It crumbled brittlely in his hand like the crumbled years that lay behind him.

He was surprised to see sunlight shining in through the windows and, as he gradually dropped the crumbled leaf, each tiny piece danced in a breeze that seemed to magically appear out of nowhere. Croome watched as the leaf bits flimsily floated throughout the room, between the curtains and out the window. Croome followed the trail of fluttering leaf crumbs to the window, drew back the curtains and stood peering out into a dazzlingly bright and beautiful fall day.

Although the trees were mostly bare, the neighborhood lawns were arrayed in their finest multicolored fall garments. Moms and dads raked the leaves into large, neat piles so that frolicking children could demolish the same piles with leaps, bounds and somersaults like acrobats in a three-ring circus. And with smiling faces, the parents cheerfully admonished their children only to watch the entire drama unfold again.

Croome noticed that Halloween decorations still adorned the neighbors' houses, and he was overjoyed. So it was still that wonderfully festive October day? His spiritual visitors had conducted their eye-opening tours all in the span of one evening. It had been a sleepless night, but an enlightening one nonetheless.

Suddenly, and without warning, Croome let out a joyous war whoop that caused the neighborhood leaf-rakers to peer up at him. They were surprised to see the formerly dour malcontent grinning like a rogue jack-o-lantern who had just met a beautiful Jill-o-lantern.

They would not have believed it if they hadn't seen it with their own eyes. A smiling Croome was a novel sight to see, the most outrageous and implausible Halloween mask on the block. When Croome saw them all staring up at him in surprise, he began laughing long and hard. He tilted his head back and laughed at the top of his lungs, rocking back and forth on his big feet like a giant punching bag. He laughed until his insides hurt and his cheeks were sore from the peculiar sensation of his lips being stretched in the opposite direction than they had become accustomed. He was most certainly out of practice when it came to the art of smiling. Fortunately, it only hurt for a short while; then it began to feel quite good. Quite good indeed.

He turned from the window to see one very wary black cat staring up at him. Croome danced over to his feline friend, scooped her up in his arms and waltzed about the room as if he was a young lover tripping the light fantastic with his dance partner. "My dear Magic. You dance divinely on this fine fall day."

And before Magic had a chance to hiss in protest, Croome deposited her padded paws upon the floor and twirled giddily toward his nightstand where he snatched up the picture of his dearly departed wife. He held it up to his newly stretched lips and gave it an audible and exaggerated smooch. "My darling Patricia. You and your hallowed friends have taught me some long overdue lessons this past evening. And for that I thank you all."

He now held the framed photo at arms length. "I promise you my darling, I am a changed man. Or, better yet, I am the old Decimus Croome who knew what it was like to be happy. I have missed you until it hurt and felt as if I had been robbed of my reason for living. Yet now I realize that I have been haunted by your memory these past agonizing years. I have been a fool, indeed. Instead of lamenting my loss, I should have been celebrating what I had… what we had"

Croome once again held the photo of his precious Patricia to his lips. "You are still my guiding light. I miss you with all my heart." He gently set down the photo and stumbled toward the stairs nearly tripping over Black Magic in his rush to set things right.

His first stop was the Home Emporium where he was greeted with a skeptical frown by a purple-aproned associate. Completely unfazed, Croome immediately grasped the startled gentleman's hand and pumped it like a carpenter pounding nails. "Good day my dear…" Croome glanced at the name-tag, for he had never bothered with names in the past. "…Clarence. And happy Halloween to you my fine friend."

Leaving the dumbfounded clerk in his wake, Croome dashed toward the holiday section of the store, a section he had despised on previous visits. This time, however, he was on a sacred mission and his grin grew broader the closer he got to the Styrofoam tombstones, giant spiders and witch's cauldrons.

Croome had forgotten all about his previous disdain for holiday trinkets and floated from one garish decoration to another as if each one was a newfound treasure waiting to be unburied. He took special delight in the talking heads and held some particularly animated conversations with mouthy monsters, pithy pirates and verbose vampires. When fellow customers shot him suspicious glances, he only responded by becoming all the more enthusiastic. "Have you ever seen so many marvelous creatures? What won't they think of next? Who would have thought a skeleton could be so witty?"

His questions were met with cautious smiles, which only encouraged him more. Placing a zombie mask over his head, he began walking stiff-legged between the aisles and approaching fellow customers with a complete lack of aplomb. "You look especially tasty my dear. You would make a delightful holiday snack."

When the recipients of the Halloween high-jinx stepped cautiously behind their shopping carts, Croome tore off the mask and pronounced, "Fear not. It is just me!!"

Upon seeing Decimus Croome, many of the startled shoppers herded their shopping carts down the nearest aisle in a desperate attempt to make a swift escape.

In quick succession, Croome morphed from a zombie, to a vampire, to an alien, to an ogre until he finally settled on a particularly suitable Frankenstein outfit and made his way to the cash register with a cart full of Halloween decorations. He held up his monster costume to the clerk and beamed with pride as he commented, "I have had way too much practice being a monster all these years, so I should be a natural at this."

The cashier agreed out of sheer bewilderment. She had indeed considered Croome a bit of a monster in years past, so she had no idea if he was being humorous or serious. It didn't matter to Croome. He was on a Halloween high and refused to let anything bring him down. He only wished he could think of an appropriately spooky song to sing as he made his way to the car with bags full of Halloween booty.

On his drive home, giddy as a trick-or-treater with a bag full of goodies, Croome veered into the local supermarket, realizing he had one more Halloween supply to purchase before heading home. Or rather, he had many more supplies to purchase, and they were all individually wrapped. After the shopping spree at the hardware store, he thought he'd seen it all. But he was in for a pleasant surprise as he entered the snack aisle of the grocery store. He was waylaid with a cornucopia of candy choices that he never knew existed. He looked warily at the never-ending bags of sweet treats veritably overflowing the shelves. He imagined being deluged by a landslide of licorice, a barrage of bubblegum, a tidal wave of toffee, or a tsunami of suckers.

"Bring it on!" He cried out to no one in particular, but attracting the attention of numerous wary shoppers. Croome began filling his basket with one bag after another of chocolates, lollipops, caramels and jellybeans. "Shall I give two to each child, or three or four?" His voice raised an octave as he exclaimed, "I will let them each grab a handful and sort it out when they get home." He finally decided as he placed the last bag of sweet treats in his overflowing shopping cart.

Croome couldn't wait for the trick-or-treaters to come to his house, so he began handing out candy on his way out of the store. "Happy Halloween!!! Merry All-Hallows Eve!!"

Some viewed him with suspicion, others with amusement, but Croome was oblivious to anything that distracted him from the tasks in front of him. He was determined to make up for all the Halloweens he had missed and especially for those he had ruined. He planned on enjoying the best Halloween ever and, more importantly, to make sure everyone he encountered also had a spectacularly festive holiday.

Croome had a couple more stops to make on his way home starting with the local hospital and bank. He was hoping to take care of some overdue payments for a friend. As he walked through the bank, he thought about that word. *Friend.* He liked the way it sounded rolling around in his head. It was a bit rusty tasting as he swirled it from side to side in his mouth, but it felt good rolling off the tongue.

"Friend." He said it out loud, ignoring the strange looks he was receiving from bank customers and employees. It was a word that he hoped to use more frequently in the years to come.

After a gratifying visit to the local hospital accounting office where he paid a few more overdue bills, Croome decided to make a stopover at Croome's Hardware store where a certain Sam Bobbich was slaving away relentlessly. Croome decided it was about time that he gave Mr. Bobbich a piece of his mind… and maybe a piece of candy while he was at it.

Upon entering the store, Croome noticed his employee was deep in discussion with a customer. When Sam looked up and saw his boss, he grew pale. He knew Decimus Croome had a strict policy regarding fraternization with the customers… …DON'T.

Sure enough, Croome approached Sam with a stern look on his face. "What is the meaning of this, Mr. Bobbich? Don't you have something better you should be doing?"

Poor Sam stuttered, "B-b-but sir, this gentleman was asking me what kind of…"

"I don't care what he was asking. I asked you if you hadn't anything better to be doing." Croome remained taciturn as he looked from the obviously annoyed customer back to the browbeaten Bobbich.

"Mr. Jenkins just stopped by to pick up some new batteries for his…" Sam started explaining to Croome before the aforementioned customer interrupted him.

"Now see here Croome. I did not come to your store just to watch you ..." As with all people in town, Bud Jenkins had seen Decimus Croome speaking rudely to Sam Bobbich on too many occasions and wasn't about to put up with anymore similar bullying tirades from the store owner.

Croome held up his hands in surrender and turned to Sam Bobbich, "Of course you have something better to be doing. It's Halloween my good gentlemen!" And now he broke into his newly rediscovered smile. "You should both be home with your families. Those trickers aren't going to treat themselves."

He looked directly at Sam and, for the first time, noticed what a kind and gentle man he had been mistreating all these years. "And as for you Sam." Croome put his hand on Sam Bobbich's shoulder. "You have a beautiful wife and two delightful young children at home. I'm sure they would love to have you with them to celebrate this joyous holiday.""

Of course Sam Bobbich was entirely speechless. He waited for the punch line to another cruel and sadistic joke. He waited for an onslaught of scolding and castigation. But it never materialized. Instead Croome linked his arm in that of Bud Jenkins and began walking him up to the cash register. "Let's get you checked out of here my fine fellow, so our friend Sam can hurry on home to his wonderful family."

"But I haven't even found the..." the customer feebly protested.

"You shouldn't be working on a holiday such as this anyway, Ben. You need to be home handing out candy to the wonderful children of this fine town."

"It's Bud. And it's much too early for trick-or-treaters."

"It's never too early for trick-or-treaters my good fellow." Said Croome as he gently ushered Mr. Jenkins out the front door. "Never too early or never too late. It's always the best time for trick-or-treaters."

Sam Bobbich was still staring in disbelief. This was not the Decimus Croome that he knew. "But Mr. Croome, who will run the store if I go home?" Sam was almost afraid to hear the answer. It had dawned on him that maybe this was his boss's demented way of terminating him.

"Who will run the store? A better question would be why is the store even open at all? Who needs hardware on Halloween? Now if we were a Halloween store, this would be the best of all days for business."

"A Halloween store?" Sam was getting more confused by the moment.

"A Halloween store!! What a great idea, Sam!! Croome's Halloween store! You're a genius. That's why you're the manager of this store."

"The manager? But Mr. Croome, I thought you..."

"You're absolutely right, Sam. Halloween only comes once a year. We'd never make a go of it as a Halloween store year-round. We'll become Croome's Holiday store. Starting tomorrow, let's make sure we're well stocked for Christmas. I do believe that's the next holiday isn't it?"

Sam Bobbich had had very little experience correcting Decimus Croome, so in a barely audible stammer he replied, "I believe Thanksgiving is the next --"

"As always, you are absolutely correct, Mr. Bobbich. It's much too early for Christmas. If we're going to be a holiday store, we'll have to focus on one holiday at a time. See, now that's why you're the manager, and that's why you're the one who's getting a big raise starting tomorrow."

"A r-r-raise?" It was not a word Sam Bobbich was accustomed to hearing.

"Yes, yes. We can talk business tomorrow. But I believe you've got a youngster at home waiting to get into his Popeye costume."

"Yes, of course…" Sam was growing ever more bewildered. "Begging your pardon Mr. Croome, but how did you know Tommy was going to wear a Popeye costume?"

"It is highly inappropriate for the manager of Croome's Holiday Store to be referring to me as Mr. Croome. From now on, it's Decimus."

"Decimus?"

"Again, you're right Sam. Way too formal. Dessy might be better." And, as with the flustered customer, Croome escorted a confused Sam Bobbich gently out the front door without so much as another word. And while at the door, Croome turned a faded old sign from **Open** to **Closed**, pulled out a jangle of keys and locked up for the remainder of a very eventful and momentous Halloween.

"Don't forget to stock up on treats at the store. Did you know they had pumpkin shaped chocolates these days?" Were the last words Sam Bobbich heard out of Mr. Cr.... Dessy's mouth as he wandered befuddled and befuzzled back to his house, his lips curled upward into a perplexed grin as he muttered to himself, "Belinda is never going to believe this."

After closing the hardware store, over two hours earlier than normal, Croome practically sprinted home in his eagerness to prepare for the big evening. His favorite feline, Black Magic, watched Croome with a wary eye as he began unpacking shopping bags and adorning the house with crazy Halloween ornaments. She batted at hanging bats, swatted at dangling spiders and hissed at glowing jack-o-lanterns.

It had been years since Croome had decorated his house for any holiday and he had no idea what should go where. "Any fool can figure out how to hang Halloween lights." He prodded himself as he looked through his abundant supply of hooks and screws and extension cords. "Especially a fool who owns a hardware store." He laughed at both his own feeble joke and at Magic's futile attempt to scare away the bobbing ghosts that were dangling from the ceiling of their front porch.

Just as the neofright had finished putting up his last set of spider-infested cobwebs, he heard a knock at the front door. "Now who can that..." Croome was only puzzled for a split second when he realized he was about to receive his first Halloween visitor.

"Oh no. The candy." He rushed into the kitchen to fill a black, plastic cauldron with mounds of treats.

He was halfway to the door when he realized, "My costume. It's Halloween, and I look just like Decimus Croome. That simply won't do." On his way to the door, he grabbed his monster mask and threw it on, backwards at first, until he bonked into an inconveniently placed wall.

A flustered Frankenstein clumsily opened his front door and blundered his way onto the porch. "Who's there? It must be a ghost. I can't see anyone." Croome's mask was still backwards, but he could hear laughter directly in front of him. He spun around in a circle as if completely befuddled. "A giggling ghost on my front porch. What sort of trickery is this?"

"You're funny." He heard the voice of a young Halloween angel who was obviously enjoying his antics.

"There is nothing funny about this." Croome snorted playfully. "I seem to have suddenly gone blind. I hear a voice, but I see no one. Oh cursed demons of Halloween.

You have stolen the eyesight of this wretched monster."

"You're mask is backwards, Mr. Monster." The angelic voice sang again.

"Mask? Backwards? What sort of sorcery is this?" Croome reached up and twisted his monster mask.

"Eegads, you're right young..." Croome stared straight in front of him, right over the head of his houseguest and at the front porch columns and leaf-strewn lawn beyond the peeling columns.

"I was right. Ghosts!! There is no one at my front porch. Only the invisible specter of a pretty princess with an enchantingly beautiful voice."

Another mischievous giggle. "Down here Mr. Monster."

"Down... Aaaah!!" Croome acted startled as he saw a young fairy princess at his door. He bowed down. "I am so sorry your highness. I was sadly mistaken. You are not a ghastly ghost but a beautiful princess. I hope you can forgive me."

Then the perky princess chanted a familiar Halloween carol that tripped off her tongue like a heavenly hymn sung by a chorus of cherubs. "Trick or treat!!"

Three more wonderful words Croome had never heard.

"I am fresh out of tricks for today, but I may just have a treat for your princessness." He swung open the screen door, reached into his cauldron of candy and scooped up a handful of goodies just in time to see the princess' mother standing on the front sidewalk shaking her head and holding up one finger.

"It appears the royal Queen Mother of Her Princessness has placed a spell upon our princess, thus I may only bequeath your highness with one magical piece of candy." Croome daintily dropped a single lollipop into the bag of the trick-or-treating royalty.

Then FrankenCroome pointed a finger at an invisible spot directly behind the fastidious Queen Mother. "Egads!! We must all hide. We are being attacked by a fire-breathing dragon."

The puzzled mother instinctively turned around to look at where Croome was pointing.

Croome took advantage of the distracted chaperone and tossed a handful of delicacies into the little princess' pink plastic trick-or-treat bag. Just as quickly, he winked at his adorable Halloween guest while the mother turned back around and shot Croome a curious look. It was a look, however, that Croome missed entirely; for the young princess bequeathed upon the poor peasant a smile that would slay any evil dragon and melt the heart of any old cranky, cantankerous curmudgeon.

Suddenly Croome was transformed, as if by magic, into the Decimus Croome of yesteryear. With that one enchanting smile, the transformation was complete. Croome fully understood the magic of Halloween. He understood the sorceress spell that came from both giving and receiving unashamedly for one extraordinarily enchanted day of the year. And he fully came to realize how that one day of sharing and charading bridged the gap between young and old and made the pendency of even the harshest winter tolerable for those who truly believed and partook to the fullest.

"Goodbye Mr. Monster." Giggled the princess as she prepared to make her royal departure. But upon reaching the bottom porch step, she turned back toward her benevolent benefactor. "And thanks for the one piece of candy." With that, she bestowed a preposterously exaggerated wink that provided the final flame to melt the last bit of choleric crankiness that coated Croome's calloused heart. A combination of holiday magic and youthful innocence proved to be every bit as powerful as even the most marvelous magic wand ever wielded by wizened wizards or wicked witches.

Gone was the *Gloom and Doom Croome* and a new Croome bloomed like a witch hazel pushing it's orange-red flowers up through the early snows of late autumn.

As the regal Princess made her way down the walkway between Croome's house and the main sidewalk, she spun around and blew Croome a kiss. He pretended to catch it before it flew over his head, and then theatrically planted it on his left monster cheek. For his splendid catch he was rewarded with a royal smile as the two new Halloween friends waved goodbye to one another.

Croome was hesitant to step back into his house, hesitant to shut the door, for he wished this moment would never end. And he may well have just stood in the doorway for hours, basking in the afterglow of this magical moment of Halloween bliss. But just then, he noticed a trio of young gentlemen walking up the sidewalk toward his house. Not wanting to spoil the whole Halloween protocol, Croome stepped inside and gently closed the door.

He felt like an exuberant child on Christmas morning and could hardly wait for his next group of trick-or-treaters. In fact, he was so giddy with anticipation; he placed his left eyeball up to the peephole on the door and watched as the trio of young revelers mounted his front porch steps. He noticed that only one of them, the smallest of the three, was in a costume. The other two boys, obviously older and clearly much taller, were dressed only in jeans and hooded sweatshirts.

None of that mattered to Croome though. He just yearned to have them ring his doorbell and chant those three magical words. The youngest boy seemed to be of the same mindset as he stretched his little hand up toward the button beside the door. But just as he was about to push it, one of the bigger boys intercepted his hand. "Not so fast you little munchkin."

"I'm not a munchkin, I'm…"

"Yeah, yeah. Whatever." The other teenager interrupted him. "You need to slow down little buddy." Now the taller of the two teenagers put his hand on the young lad's shoulder in a conspiratorial sort of way. Just about then, Croome recognized both of the bigger fellows. They had visited him last year at Halloween and weren't too pleased with the carrots and celery he handed out.

Croome held no grudge against them; in fact he felt bad. He had definitely been a Halloween Grinch in years past. But he was going to make it up this year. Or at least he wanted to make it up, if only this trio of trick-or-treaters would ring the doorbell or knock on the door or…

Just as Croome was about to lose his patience and open the door, he heard the taller boy continue his speech to the little guy. "Okay now, this guy is the best treater in the whole neighborhood."

"Really?" Gasped the little fella, his eyes growing as wide as Croome's candy cauldron.

"Would I lie to my little brother" Asked the older boy as he shot his other non-costumed conspirator a sly grin.

"Well sometimes you…"

"Shut up and listen. So like I was saying, this guy is the best Halloween treater in town. But sometimes he has to be reminded how nice he is. So no matter what he throws in your bag, here's what you have to do." At this point, the older brother leaned down low so that his crew cut head was on level with his little brother's mask. Then he whispered something in his younger sibling's ear.

"But Mom said…"

"But Mom said." The other boy whined, mocking the youngster. "Do you see your mom around here anywhere?" He looked from the little brother to the big brother. "Cause I don't see her anywhere. She ain't never trick-or-treated at this guy's house. So she don't know nothin' about this whole Halloween thing. That's why she sent us with you. We're here to teach you the proper way to trick-or-treat." He said 'proper' with a horrible British accent.

"Well okay." The little guy decided. "But will you two stay here with me?"

"We'll be right down here in the bushes." The big brother joined back in the conversation. "Most people don't like big kids trick-or-treating, and we don't want to cramp your style. You know, maybe he won't give you as much candy if we're with you. But don't worry; we'll be right here."

And with that, the two big boys jumped down into the bushes and gave each other a high five. "Good luck kid." Blue shirt muttered, and they both laughed and fist-bumped each other.

Finally, Croome heard the delightful jangle of the doorbell as the little boy stood on his toes and pressed the button with the very tip of an outstretched finger.

When Croome opened the door, he could see the boy was dressed in some type of kung fu reptile outfit that looked only vaguely recognizable. Before the door was even halfway opened, Croome heard his second "Trick-or-treat" of the evening and nearly cried out in joy. Oh those magically marvelous words.

"You must be a magical wizard turtle." Croome reached into his cauldron of treats. "How else could you climb all the way up onto my porch and ring my doorbell?"

"I'm not a wizard." The boy struck a karate chop pose. "I'm a ninja."

"Well of course you are," Croome nodded. "That was going to be my next guess. He held a fistful of candy over the boy's trick-or-treat bag and dumped it in, like a toy crane dumping its load of goodies into a bin.

At this point, Croome could hear the two older boys snickering in the bushes, no doubt thinking that Croome had dropped a handful of vegetables into the bag, as in years past.

"Thanks!!" Said the young boy. In his excitement, he nearly turned around and bounded off the porch. But then he remembered his brother's whispered instructions. He turned back to Croome and repeated, "Please sir," He stuck out his lower lip as if pouting. "May I have another?"

Now Croome could hear the older boys trying hard to stifle their laughter but miserably failing.

"May you have another?" Croome asked, aiming his question more toward the big boys in the bushes than the little boy on the porch. "May you have another?"

Then Croome reached his big paws into the cauldron of goodies and scooped not one but two handfuls of treats into the little boy's bag. "You're in the wrong story my young friend, but you can have as much as you'd like."

"Wow!!!" The little boy looked into his bag and was nearly blinded by the dazzling beauty of his favorite candy bars staring back up at him. "My brother was right. You're the nicest man on the block." With that he spun on his reptilian heels and ran toward the edge of the porch. As he stepped down onto the top porch step, he remembered his manners and turned back to Croome. "Thanks mister. My brother was right about you. You're awesome."

Croome was amused to see, through the thick foliage beside his porch, two huge sets of eyes staring at him in disbelief. He hollered at the turtle shell on the back of the little trick-or-treater. "Tell your brother that I've got plenty of treats for him too. And his friend." With that, Croome tossed a handful of candy into the bushes beside his porch and waved at his incognito visitors.

As the night wore on, robots, ghosts, ninjas, witches, superheroes and demons visited FrankenCroome. Each of them received high praise for their creative and delightful costumes. Each also received an abundance of Halloween treats. But Croome was the one whose bounty was the richest; for with each chant of 'trick-or-treat', each smiling face, each youthful 'thank you,' the new and improved Croome gained a greater appreciation for the joys of the Halloween spirit.

Croome would have been happy to remain at his house, providing treats for his visitors of all ages. He cared not whether they were youngsters or teenagers. Whether they were costumed crusaders or plain-clothes revelers. For no costume, no matter how intricate or elaborate, was as uplifting as the smiles worn by the beguiling beggars.

Four spirits had visited Croome on this hallowed day, and he carried each of those spirits with him and in him. And as a result, his own spirit had been reinvigorated. And it was this new and improved spirit that had one final Halloween house to haunt.

# Chapter 13 – Franken Croome

Leaving a black cauldron on his porch, filled to overflowing with sweet treats, Croome set out on a journey to right the wrongs of Halloween past. With a pocket full of treats, a heart full of joy and a monster mask on his head, Croome lumbered down familiar streets and marauded through long-forgotten neighborhoods on his way toward his final act of attrition.

As he journeyed, he greeted and treated each wee warlock, mini monster and diminutive demon with a treat from his bottomless pockets. He shouted out Halloween greetings to every house he passed and cautioned drivers to beware of costumed creatures crossing the streets. Croome embraced the last day of October like a father embraces his long lost prodigal son and was even more generous with his spirit than he was with his candy.

Finally he reached his destination, one particularly popular residence crawling with costumed revelers and overflowing with the sounds of Halloween ballads about werewolves, zombies and purple people eaters. Approaching the house, Croome lifted his monster mask and delighted at the festive and macabre decorations festooned about the exterior. On the porch alone his eyes were greeted by a giant spider suspended in a sea of gossamer webbing, an evil looking skeleton, at least a half dozen jack-o-lanterns of all shapes and sizes and squatting gargoyles with blazing eyes.

Homemade ghosts hung from every tree and shrub while orange and black lights illuminated the awnings and doorways. A gigantic banner hung over the entryway with the words ENTER IF YOU DARE printed in gothic font, faux-blood dripping from each letter.

Although his daughter had expended herculean efforts to represent their residence as a chillingly spooky haunted house, the true mood was quite the opposite as the joyous laughter and squeals of children spilled out of the house and flooded the neighborhood. Croome was so excited to join the party that he nearly forgot to put on his Frankenstein mask. □

Lumbering up the steps then taking one last moment to check his fiendish attire, Croome cautiously made his way into the house. At first he expected all heads to turn and stare at him gape-jawed from amazement. But he quickly realized that he was just another masked monster at the monster's ball. As of yet, no one had the least idea who he was nor any reason to suspect that it might be the local demon brought back to life by the Spirits of Halloween.

Croome had never seen so many clever and creative costumes in his life. He had no idea who many of them were intended to be, but he was impressed nonetheless. Of course there were a good many costumes that he did recognize, and he received great joy in seeing some of the old standards. He recognized superheroes and super-villains as he was bumped by a Batman, jostled by a Joker, and nearly pummeled by a Penguin. Croome joyfully forgave each transgression and was, in turn, forgiven his own clumsy lumbering. If only such spirit prevailed year round he thought to himself.

Just then a young vampiress displaying more underwear than overbite walked past Croome and into a large crowd of costumed teens. Croome noticed that all the girls were short on costume and long on cleavage, and he grinned as he thought back to his sister's comparatively innocent Halloween outfit of many years past. He smiled even broader when he imagined what his own mother would think of these modern teen costumes.

As if on cue, he heard a familiar voice from the crowd. At first he didn't recognize her, but then he realized his own sister was standing only a few short feet away. She was dressed as some kind of werewolf or demon wolf or something everyone else in the room knew about except Decimus Croome. She was sternly gesturing to one of the young teen girls in the crowd.

It was obvious, even to Croome, that the teenage girl was supposed to be Little Bo Peep. She had the shepherd's crook, the curly golden hair and a semi-Bo Peepish dress on. But this particular Bo Peep was missing more than just her sheep. She seemed to also be missing large portions of her costume from the top and bottom of her baby-blue dress.

Bo Peep rolled her eyes and grudgingly moped over toward the scowling wolf. As she drew nearer, Croome recognized the scantily clad shepherdess. It was his very own niece. Why he hadn't seen young Annie Blevins in years. She looked much less like the little niece he remembered and much more like the precocious sister he remembered. In fact, he was flabbergasted to realize that she looked exactly like a young teenage Tessa.

Neither mother nor daughter had any idea that their brother and uncle was scrutinizing them as they squared off for battle.

"That is not the costume that we bought you." Tessa Croome huffed, pointing her finger directly at her daughter's boobs.

Ann rolled her eyes and looked up at the ceiling. "Yes it is, *Mother*." The emphasis on 'Mother.'

"I do *not* think so, *Daughter*." The gauntlet had been thrown, the challenge accepted. The emphasis was on both 'not' and 'Daughter.'

"Yes it is." Emphasis on 'is.' "I just made some modifications."

"Some modifications. I expected to see you in a cute Little Bo Peep outfit. Since when did Little Bo Peep become a slut?"

"There's no need to talk like that Mother!!"

Croome immediately flashed back to a Halloween over twenty years ago when Tessa had been on the receiving end of the 'slutty costume' debate. He was glad to be wearing a mask, because Frankenstein's ugly mug was hiding an absolutely huge grin.

The big, bad mama wolf looked like she was about to devour poor innocent little Bo Peep. "I have no idea where your sheep are little Miss Peep, but I can tell you that they aren't what's sticking out of the skimpy little top you're wearing."

The dialogue had grown a tad bit spicier over the years, but the mother-daughter debate was the same. Decimus had been too young to notice the subtle nuances on that long-ago Halloween, but he was devouring them now. Young Ann's tone was a mixture of anger, contempt and exasperation while Tessa's tone dripped with sarcasm, disbelief and, Croome detected, a subtle undertone of jealousy at the budding youth she would never see again.

"That is just sick, Mom." Croome noticed a slight variation in tactics. The angrily spoken *Mother* had become a gentler *Mom*. Not only had Ann changed the words and the tone, she had also changed her battle plan.

And Croome was loving it.

But the Mama Wolf wasn't backing down. "I'll tell you what's sick. That outfit on a sixteen year old girl at a neighborhood party is what's sick." Absolutely no retreat from the reformed Halloween tart as she picked up a head of steam. "Why when I was your age, my mother would have never let me wear a costume like that."

Croome could bear it no longer. He let out a huge snort, loud enough to draw the attention of those nearby... including his sister and niece.

They both turned to look at him. In a split second, the two verbal warriors turned from mortal enemies to collaborating combatants. They confronted him with slightly different variations of the same evil glare. Whereas Tessa looked at him as if he was cockroach in need of stomping, Ann's glare made it clear that she thought he was some rude old pervert.

"Excuse me?!" Tessa Blevins-Formerly-Croome took a step toward him, the mama wolf protecting her cub.

Croome almost took off his mask, but decided to have a little fun as he addressed his irate sister. "I don't blame you for being so mad. I bet you never would have worn a Halloween costume like that when you were young."

There was a moment of hesitation from Tessa Croome who recognized the voice behind that monster mask, but couldn't quite make the connection. "*That* is none of your business!!" Emphasis on *That*.

"You're absolutely right." Croome said, from behind his protective monster mask. He was just warming up.

Croome started to turn away, then turned back toward his sister. "Besides, even if you would have wanted to wear a costume like that, I bet your mother would have never allowed it."

Now Tessa was positive that she should know who this monst… this person was. There was something exceedingly familiar about the voice, the swagger, the smugness. "There is no way my mom would have let me wear a costume like that…"

"And I'm sure you wouldn't have snuck out of the house and worn *a costume like that* anyway?"

Ann looked about ready to jump to her mom's defense when teenage curiosity and defiance kicked in. "Wait a minute." Ann turned from glaring at FrankenCroome to a slightly more inquisitive glare at her mother. "If you said your mother wouldn't let you wear a costume like that, then that means you must have tried to wear one." The focus of the conversation had shifted away from Ann's costume, and she wasn't about to let it shift back. "So what kind of costumes did you wear when you were my age, Mom?"

"Well... I..." Tessa was flustered and brother Croome was thoroughly enjoying the shifting tides of battle. "Well, she was my mother, so I..."

All of the sudden Tessa realized that she was being double teamed and rounded on the interloping monster. "I don't know who you are, but this is none of your business. Maybe you should just go eavesdrop somewhere else."

She had no idea that it was her brother behind the monstrous mask and that his mischievous grin was about to split that mask in two. But when he didn't move or respond, Tessa got even more angry.

"Listen buddy. If you don't get out of here, I'll go get my husband and..."

Croome reached into his pocket and pulled out the remaining candy. "I'll give you all my candy if you don't tell anyone our little secret." He was of course referring to the exact same bribe his sister had offered him on that Halloween so many years ago. That Halloween was fresh in his mind since he and a certain Spirit of Halloween Past had just visited it the previous evening.

Tessa was confused at first. Not only did the voice

sound familiar, but she knew she had heard those exact words somewhere else. But since they were spoken so many Halloweens ago, she was having trouble making the connection.

Like a tag-team wrestler, Ann was ready to jump into the ring. Only this time her target was the tall, green stranger. There wasn't a single mask in the room that was as horrifying as a teenager's evil glare, and Little Bo Creep was pointing her ultimate weapon at big, bad FrankenCroome now. "You are *disgusting Mister.*" emphasis on both disgusting and Mister. "Who are you anyway? Maybe it's time for you to find another party to crash. Who invited you, anyway?"

"As a matter of fact, I believe it was that handsome vampire over there." FrankenCroome said, pointing to Darren Tate who was watching his son bob for apples.

As Croome spoke to his niece, his sister slowly began to recognize his voice and mannerisms. She took one step closer to him, and her tone became much less confrontational as she slowly came to realize who she was looking at. In a voice that barely rose above a whisper, she uttered, "It couldn't be." Then just a bit louder, "There's no way."

Now Tessa's daughter was looking from the perverted monster to her mother, then back again as if she was watching some bizarre tennis match. "What in the f..."

"Fudge knuckles." Both Decimus & Tessa said, at the same time.

"Oh my God!!!" Tessa nearly screamed as she realized why the irritating stranger seemed so familiar. "It can't be."

The monster and wolf slowly walked toward each other, bridging the years of separation with each step. And at long last, the two disparate creatures shared a warm and long-overdue embrace.

Nearby, Ann stared at the two hugging Halloween creatures. "Okay, this is the creepiest Halloween **Ever**." Huge emphasis on **Ever**.

Ann wasn't the only one to notice. As the two Croome siblings shared a long, warm and hearty embrace, all eyes were on them. It was obvious something had just happened. But it was a complete Halloween puzzle as to what it was.

New friends, old friends, neighbors and classmates, all dressed in Halloween oddities, gathered around as if drawn by some magnetic force. When Decimus looked up, the first group he recognized was the Bobbich family. He immediately recognized Popeye, Brutus and Olive Oyl but hadn't the least idea who young Kate was supposed to be.

Then he spied his brother-in-law and grandson. And, as if from far away, he heard a familiar voice that filled his heart with joy.

"Excuse me. What's going on? How come no one is playing games anymore? Why is Everyone..." Eve Tate stopped short. She had seen a lot of wild and wacky things at the yearly Halloween parties, but never anything quite like this. In the center of the crowd were two hugging creatures, a monster and a werewolf. The werewolf appeared to be her Aunt Tessa. But who was the monster? Something about him looked familiar.

Then, as if he read her mind, FrankenCroome parted from the werewolf and started clumsily lumbering, toward her. As if in a Halloween fog, he gradually reached up to the top of his head and slowly pulled off his mask.

Surely it couldn't be her father. Decimus Croome did not do Halloween parties. Decimus Croome did not do parties of any kind. And Decimus Croome... her father...

did not dress up in monster costumes and hug werewolves. The father of her dreams did those things. But not her real father. Not the real Decimus Croome.

Yet here he was. Standing right in front of her, monster mask in his hand, and a huge smile in the middle of his face. She tried to remember if she'd ever seen him smile before and could not think of one instance.

Until now.

Here he was. A smiling Decimus Croome. A costumed Decimus Croome.

The vampire makeup she had spent over an hour applying was rapidly disappearing in a torrent of tears. White tears spilled over onto red lips and dropped off jagged plastic teeth. She had heard stories, more like long-lost legends, that her father had once been a fun-loving, cheerful human being. That was the father she'd always dreamed of, ever since she was a little girl. She stubbornly wanted to believe that her real father was hiding somewhere inside the crabby old curmudgeon that greeted her each day after school - the one who ruined Halloween each year. She desperately prayed that some evil sorcerer had cast a spell on her real daddy and, if she hoped and prayed each day, maybe, just maybe, the spell would be broken and she would be granted her real father back.

But as the sweet little Eve grew into the teenage Eve, and the teenage Eve into the adult Eve, she began to believe her dream to be a fantasy. Witches and sorcerers only came out at Halloween, and they weren't real. Dreams were just dreams until they became nightmares. Not the *fall off a cliff getting devoured by monsters* type nightmares but the everyday nightmares that devoured dreams and gradually became a reality. Could nightmares turn back to dreams? Could dreams come true on some enchanted Halloween?

"Dad?"

One large monster tear flowed from each of Decimus Croome's eyes. "Eve." He stretched his long arms toward his daughter. They were the long and loving arms of a father, not the stiff and clumsy limbs of a Halloween monster.

Eve's petite hands were lost in her father's monstrous palms. Like a jolt of electricity entering Frankenstein's neck bolts, an energy far greater than any electrical current passed between Father and Daughter. At first they could only stare at each other through tearful eyes. Their smiles were the envy of every costumed clown in the crowd as they came together in a long-overdue embrace.

Decimus Croome whispered into his daughter's ear. "I am so sorry. I am sorry for all the missed Halloweens and ruined holidays. I'm sorry I wasn't the father you deserved. Can you ever forgive me?"

Eve looked at her father, and it was as if an evil spell had been lifted. Could it be possible that the cranky, miserly father she had known all these years was gone and was replaced with the father of her dreams? "We have lots of Halloweens in front of us, Dad." Was all she could say. But there were so many other things she wanted to say.

"I promise," Decimus Croome vowed. "I promise to be the best father any girl ever had."

Costumed partiers began dispersing to partake in the Halloween themed activities set up around the house. Young Kellen Tate, who seemed oblivious to the momentous events that had transpired on this magical evening, squealed with delight as his father the vampire chased him in circles around his mother and grandfather.

Eve looked back in the direction of her father. "Best father and grandfather?" She asked.

Before Decimus Croome could answer, Belinda Bobbich approached with Tommy clinging to her hand. Eve and Decimus both smiled at the sight of such a cute Olive Oyl and Popeye duo.

Belinda apologized for interrupting the conversation, then addressed her former adversary. "I never thought I would say this Mr. Croome…"

Croome interrupted her. "Please call me Dessy. Or at least Decimus."

"That may take some getting used to." Belinda returned his smile. "I never thought I would say this but I think you deserve an award for best boss of the year."

In a crowd of shocked bystanders, Decimus may have been the most stunned of everyone. He had only recently realized what a truly horrible boss he had been. And now, one of his harshest critics was praising him.

Belinda continued. "When we got a call from the hospital saying that someone had paid our medical bills, I thought there was some mistake." She looked down at her son and squeezed his hand. "Then, when we got another call from the bank saying that someone had also paid our overdue house payments, I was completely floored. I no longer thought it was a mistake, but I started to believe in angels. Then when Sam told me about his promotion and pay raise, I started to realize who the angel was. And it was the person who I would have least suspected."

Croome reached down and rubbed Tommy's shiny head. "I'm not sure about an angel, but there must be someone out there who knows what a wonderful young man…" Croome stopped talking and looked around the room at Sam, Belinda and Kate. "What a wonderful family you are."

Tommy wasn't quite sure what the adults were talking about, but it had been a long time since he had seen his mom look so happy. And he had never seen a smile on Decimus Croome's face.

Croome changed the subject before things got too mooshy. "I've been thinking about retiring for a long time." He looked at his daughter. "It would be nice to spend a little more time with my grandson."

Sam Bobbich peeled himself away from the bobbing-for-apples group and walked over to join his wife. Croome took the opportunity to make a proposal he had been considering. "I know I can trust this man to run the store."

He placed a beefy hand on Sam's shoulder. "But I bet he could use some help keeping the old place going." Now he glanced toward his daughter. "I'd love to hand the family business over to the next generation."

Eve looked genuinely stunned for the second time that evening. "I have no idea how to run a hardware store." She also didn't remember any *take your daughter to work days* but refrained from commenting on that particular subject.

"Who said anything about a hardware store? It seems like we already have one too many of those in town anyway." Croome raised his eyebrows and glanced from Eve to Sam. Then, with one hand still on Sam's shoulder he placed the other hand on his daughter's shoulder. "Enough business talk for now. You two can iron out the details later. In the meantime, I believe there's a pack of Halloween goblins preparing to attack us."

And with that, little Tommy Bobbich and Kellen came running over and grabbed Grampa Croome by the hands. They led him toward the Pin-the-Tale-on-the-Werewolf game and fitted him with a blindfold. Spinning him around, they laughed hysterically as he pinned the tale on everything except the werewolf.

Decimus Croome spent the next hour playing every Halloween game in the house. He broke balloons, ate squirmy worms, decorated haunted house cookies and bobbed for apples. By the end of the party, he had never been so tired nor so contented in his life.

Darren Tate, his booming voice rising above the din, announced that it was time for the Dracademy Awards. Eve leaned over toward her father. "The Dracademy Awards are…"

Her father interrupted. "Oh I know all about the famous Dracademy Awards."

She looked at him with a puzzled expression. "How could you possibly know about…"

Croome smiled. "Let's just say I've had some very spirited friends visiting me, and they taught me a thing or two about Halloween."

Eve had no idea what her father was talking about, but after all the strange happenings of this evening, she wasn't the least bit surprised by one more oddity.

After the awards ceremony, Croome played more Halloween games with his grandson and Tommy Bobbich. Before long it appeared that the party was starting to wind down, so Decimus sat back in a big comfortable chair, scooped Tommy onto one knee and Kellen onto the other and gave them both a big monster hug.

"Will you come to our Halloween party next year, Grampa?" asked Kellen.

"I will never miss another Halloween party as long as I live." Promised Decimus Croome.

And he meant it.

He looked around at the guests, some still playing games and others preparing to depart. He found himself wishing it was Halloween every night. For way too many years he had viewed this holiday night with ignorant disdain. But he now realized what he had missed and wanted to make up for lost time.

---

As Croome walked home that evening, he realized that he was already looking forward to next Halloween and the one after that. A chilly gust of wind settled into his bones, and he couldn't help but appreciate the crisp fall night. The last of the colorful leaves dropped silently about him, and he thought about how Halloween was the perfect autumn holiday. People were much like leaves on the trees. In the comfortably warm summer, they were verdant and supple. But then autumn rolled around each year, and they donned their brightly colored Halloween costumes for one last wild party. Then, when fall was over, the trees stood bare, revealed for all to see and appreciated all the more for what they had been.

Croome sighed to think that he nearly missed his chance to celebrate life's grandest party. It would be a long winter, but the memories of this joyous Halloween would see him through to a brand new spring and a new life filled with family and friends. He vowed that he would never let another Halloween go by without donning his most outrageous and flamboyant Halloween costume and celebrating another year of life and living to the fullest. Sometimes, he realized, it is our costumes that show who we really are.

Just before he reached home, a rather frigid breeze churled about him kicking up a whirlwind of chattering leaves. As Croome fastened the very top button of his jacket, he thought he heard a voice coming from the swirling leaves. "Happy Halloween, Decimus." It seemed to sigh with a particularly soothing and familiar voice.

"Happy Halloween to you too Patricia." Croome replied to the wind. Then he hastened to add, "And happy birthday too. Maybe you can come back and visit me on Thanksgiving or, better yet, at Christmas."

He heard only the sound of the wind dying back down and depositing its precious cargo of autumn leaves on the ground. At first Croome felt a sense of loneliness, until he realized that he would never truly be alone again.

With that thought, Decimus Croome began to laugh. "Pish posh and poppycock. Spirits visiting at Christmas? Whoever heard of ghosts at Christmas?" As he walked onto the porch of his newly decorated home with the nearly empty cauldron near the door, he was certain he could hear the spirits of Halloween laughing right along with him.

29961127R00155

Made in the USA
Columbia, SC
25 October 2018